THE GOLDEN MOONS OF
JUPITER
ANTHONY FUCILLA

Published 2022 by arima publishing

www.arimapublishing.com

ISBN 978 1 84549 *** *

© Anthony Fucilla 2022

Typeset in Garamond

Swirl is an imprint of arima publishing.

arima publishing
ASK House, Northgate Avenue
Bury St Edmunds, Suffolk IP32 6BB
t: (+44) 01284 700321

www.arimapublishing.com

Contents

OTHER BOOKS BY THE AUTHOR

Novellas

THE MARS TIME-PROJECT

BEYOND EARTH'S HORIZON

Short story books

QUANTUM CHRONICLES
IN THE ELEVENTH DIMENSION

QUANTUM CHRONICLES 2

IMPERIAL PLANET

SILENT EARTH

ANDROIDS AND THE GODS

The Golden Moons of Jupiter

Anthony Fucilla

We are the consciousness
of the universe.

Time to conquer the stars...

The Golden Moons of Jupiter

Chapter 1

Dabrowski's eyes, a shade of hazel, expressed both confidence and brilliance. He let his gaze roam and said, "You've got to be believers."

All the members of the government committee sat there, fully attentive, as probing beams of sunlight shone into the hall. It was a piercing white day.

"There are approximately seventy-nine moons within the Jupiter system, collectively referred to as the Jovians, Ganymede being the largest. Ganymede, Europa and Callisto are known to have interior oceans at, or near, their core-mantle boundary. The presence of oceans is not only considered an indication of potential life on these particular moons but is also cited as a reason for possible human habitation. Now, there are several proposals on how we could go about terraforming these moons with the aim of making them suitable for human settlement."

"Professor Dabrowski," muttered one of the elderly men from the committee, his strong polished English accent standing out boldly in the company of the Americans. "Please forgive my early interruption but the point I'd like to make at this juncture is... why should we, the people of Earth, waste energy, time and money on something that is really not necessary as far as I'm concerned? We should be more focused on the future and well-being of our own planet. Terraforming the Moons of Jupiter sounds fantastic and intriguing as an idea, especially for lovers of science fiction, but I think it's a concept that's best left there."

Dabrowski looked the speaker directly in the eye. He had expected some of the committee to exhibit this type of narrow-mindedness.

"Sir, with all due respect you need to look at this more philosophically. It's the great pioneers, the explorers that changed our world and made it what it is today... the likes of Christopher Columbus, Giovanni Caboto, Marco Polo and so forth. The same spirit that drove them drives many like me in search of further conquest, further discovery. It's this driving force that leads to greater understanding. We are the consciousness of the universe."

He paused and then addressed the whole room again.

"Now on a more practical level, terraforming is important because Earth is becoming overpopulated. Thus colonizing and terraforming could help us solve this issue. It will give us, the people of Earth, the chance to migrate and settle on these future worlds."

The previous speaker and the rest of the committee sat there mutely. Dabrowski sighed and continued.

"Now, when it comes to exploration, terraforming and settlement, each moon presents its own share of advantages and of course, disadvantages. These are: its proximity to Jupiter, each moon's particular structure and composition, the availability of water and finally, whether or not the moon in question is dominated by Jupiter's powerful magnetic field. So, with regard to terraforming and the possible methods involved, in short, it's all about leveraging the indigenous resources and the moons' own interactions with Jupiter's magnetic field to create an atmosphere that is breathable."

"But surely that's an impossible mission Professor?" snapped one of the ladies from the committee.

"Please let me finish madam. In terms of the process, it would start by heating the surface in order to sublimate the ice, a process which could involve orbital mirrors. These mirrors would basically focus sunlight onto the surface. This in turn would generate heat, maximizing sunlight absorption and thus help to terraform. Another way to generate heat would be to use nuclear detonators, or by crashing comets and meteors into the surface. Once the surface ice begins to melt, it would form dense clouds of water vapour and gaseous volatiles such as carbon dioxide, ammonia and methane. These would create a greenhouse effect. Furthermore, the exposure of water vapour to Jupiter's radiation would result in the creation of hydrogen and oxygen gas. Hydrogen would escape into space while oxygen would remain closer to the surface. This process actually occurs around Ganymede, Callisto and Europa and is responsible for their tenuous atmospheres which contain oxygen gas. And since ammonia is mainly composed of nitrogen, it could be converted into nitrogen gas via the introduction of certain strains of bacteria. With nitrogen acting as a buffer gas, a nitrogen-oxygen atmosphere with enough air pressure to sustain humans could be created."

The lady adjusted her specs and began to type away briskly on her minicomputer, making notes. A sudden, piercing electronic shriek emanated from her device, almost like an overloaded distorted time signal. Dabrowski frowned. It had broken the flow of his delivery. He gathered his thoughts and continued...

"Another interesting and fascinating option is 'para-terraforming.' Basically, it's a process where a world such as Ganymede, Callisto, or Europa, is enclosed in an artificial shell in order to transform its environment. This would involve building huge Shell Worlds to encase them. Keeping the atmospheres inside long enough will inevitably cause long-term changes. Furthermore, within such shells, Ganymede, Callisto and Europa could have their temperatures slowly raised as time elapses. The water-vapor atmospheres could be exposed to ultra-violet radiation from internal UV lights and bacteria could then be introduced. Other elements could be added as needed."

There was a brief pause while Dabrowski marshalled his thoughts for the next stage of his presentation. The committee members took the moment to whisper amongst themselves but at this stage he could not tell if they were positive or negative. Dabrowski, his eyes full of zeal and energy, rubbed his jaw, and said, "Now with regard to colonizing and terraforming Europa, I'd like to give you a detailed, focused explanation. Its orbit is nearly circular, with an eccentricity of 0.09 and lies at an average distance of 670,900 km from the gas giant Jupiter. It takes Europa 3.55 Earth days to complete a single orbit. Furthermore, this Moon, currently a deserted ball of frozen liquid and hydrothermal vents, is one that can without any doubt be terraformed because of its abundant water, which comes in both solid and liquid form.

Using nuclear devices and impacts from comets and asteroids to increase surface temperature, Europa's surface ice could be sublimated and form a great atmosphere of water vapor. Once this vapor is exposed to Jupiter's magnetic field, it would then undergo radiolysis, converting into oxygen gas which would remain and hydrogen that would escape into space. Via this complex process the result would be the creation of an ocean world. Floating settlements could then be constructed. Now because

Europa is tidally-locked, these colonies could move from the day-side to the night-side in order to create the illusion of a diurnal cycle.

The ocean itself probably contains organic molecules, oxygenated and heated by Europa's geologically active core and as a result of these factors, there is a strong possibility that organic life exists in this ocean, perhaps in microbial or even multi-celled form."

"Next, I'd like to consider Ganymede... It is the largest moon in the Solar-System, even larger than planet Mercury and like most moons, it too is tidally locked, with one side always facing toward the planet. Ganymede orbits at an average distance of 1,070,400 km, varying from 1,069,200 km at periapsis to at 1,071,600 km apoapsis. At this particular distance, it takes seven days and three hours to complete a single revolution. Composition-wise, Ganymede is mainly composed of water ice and silicate rock. Now, more importantly Ganymede can be terraformed for the following reasons... Ganymede has a gravitational force of 1.428 m/s2 which is comparable to Earth's Moon and sufficient to limit the effects of bone and muscle degeneration. This lower gravity also means that the moon has a lower escape velocity which, in turn, means it would take considerably less fuel for rockets to take off from the surface.

Furthermore, the presence of a magnetosphere means that the colonists would be better shielded from highly energetic particles in the form of lethal cosmic radiation than on other bodies like the moons Io and Europa. In fact, Ganymede receives approximately 8 rem of radiation per day. That's a significant reduction from Io and Europa, but still well above human tolerance. The fact that Ganymede is mainly composed of water ice means that colonists could also produce breathable oxygen, not to mention their own drinking water, and would be able to synthesise rocket fuel. This can be achieved by heating up the surface of the moon through various means, sublimating the water ice and allowing radiolysis to convert it into oxygen. The end result would be the creation of an ocean world.

Furthermore, like Europa there is a distinct possibility that Ganymede has an interior ocean due to the heat created by tidal flexing in its mantle. Via hydrothermal vents this heat could be transferred into the water. In turn this could provide the required heat and energy to sustain life. Finally, combined with oxygenated water, life forms could indeed exist at the core-mantle boundary in the form of Extremophiles. Extremophiles are organisms that live in extreme environments under high pressure and temperature."

He paused trying to gauge the room but there were no indications yet of what conclusions the committee might reach. Remaining composed, he continued...

"So, we come to Callisto... This moon is the outermost of the Galileans, orbiting Jupiter at an average distance of 1,882,700 km. It is the second largest of Jupiter's moons and the third largest satellite in the solar system. Callisto presents multiple advantages as far as colonization is concerned. It has an abundant supply of water beneath the surface, much like the others. However, unlike the others, Callisto's distance from Jupiter means that colonists would have far less to worry about in terms of radiation. In fact, with a surface exposure of about 0.01 rem a day Callisto is well within human tolerances. However, it is important to note that the environmental conditions necessary for life to appear, which includes the presence of enough heat due to tidal flexing, are more likely on Ganymede and Europa. The main difference is the lack of contact between the rocky material and the interior ocean, as well as the lower heat flux in Callisto's interior. In essence, while Callisto possesses the necessary pre-biotic chemistry to host life, it lacks the necessary energy.

In terms of terraforming Callisto... just like Ganymede and Europa, the method would involve heating up the surface in order to sublimate the surface ice and create an atmosphere which produces oxygen through radiolysis. As a result, the world produced would be an ocean planet that reached to depths of between approximately 130 and 351 km."

A youngish looking gentleman with a full head of neatly arranged hair suddenly raised his hand and muttered, "Professor you have covered the potential methods with exquisite detail, and it has certainly been interesting, I might say fascinating, but could you touch on the potential difficulties that we face in terms of terraforming and creating an environment on these moons?"

"Of course. They are as follows... distance, natural hazards, resources and infrastructure, sustainability and of course, the ethical considerations. In short the Jovian system is very far from our planet, planet Earth. On average the distance between here and Jupiter is 628,411,977 million km. Furthermore, any vessels transporting human crews to the Jovian system would likely have to rely on cryogenics, freezing, or hibernation-related tech in order to be faster, smaller and of course more cost effective. Transport missions to and from the Asteroid Belt could be equipped with systems like nuclear-thermal propulsion, fusion-drive systems, or some other highly advanced complex system. But thus far, no such drive systems exist..."

"I see," said the man, his dark eyes focused and intense.

"Another important thing to mention here is the need for refuelling and supply stations between Earth and the Jovian System... like an outpost on the Moon, a permanent base on the red planet Mars and bases on Ceres and in the Asteroid Belt."

There was a moment of silence. It seemed to drag. Dabrowski drew himself straight and continued...

"Radiation is, of course, another obstacle. In fact, radiation would be a huge problem for humans living on Europa or Ganymede but not Callisto. As previously mentioned, with a surface exposure of about 0.01 rem a day, Callisto is well within human tolerances. Thus any settlements established on Europa and Ganymede would require radiation shielding, even after the creation of viable atmospheres. Huge shields would have to be built in orbit of the moons. Another concern for the future colonists would be the danger of space rocks slamming into their ocean world, not to mention the problems of adjusting to a much weaker gravitational field. The weak gravity on each of those moons, Ganymede, Europa and Callisto could cause long term health problems and even affect the biochemistry of the body, including the mind.

Now with regard to the issue of sustainability... sustainability has to do with the fact that all of the Jovian moons either lack a magnetosphere or, in the case of Ganymede, are not powerful enough to block the effects of

Jupiter's powerful magnetic field. As a result of this, any atmosphere created would be slowly stripped away. In order to maintain the effects of terraforming, the colonists would need to replenish the atmosphere over time.

Terraforming and colonising Callisto, Europa and Ganymede would result in the creation of three ocean worlds that varied in terms of depth from 100km in the case of Europa to extreme depths of up to 800 km in the case of Ganymede. These water worlds with extremely deep oceans will inevitably cause complications for the colonists. For example with oceans that deep, all settlements would have to take the form of floating cities that could not be anchored to solid ground. This raises the logical question of... would it even be possible to build stable floating cities? Or would they be swallowed up by huge tidal waves? Or worse yet, swept off into the emptiness of space by waves so brutally high, they slipped the bonds of the moon's gravitational field? This all sounds fantastic, but these are some of the realistic challenges we could face.

Finally, it would be remiss of me not to mention the ethics of terraforming.... Many Scientists believe there is indigenous life on one or more of the Jovian moons, thus the effects of terraforming and colonising could have severe consequences for them. If bacterial life forms exist on the underside of Europa's icy surface, then melting it would mean death for these organisms. Melting the ice would remove their only source of protection from the brutal radiation. The presence of man alone could cause problems. Germs, organisms, introduced by humans to the alien worlds could cause a devastating chain reaction. However, it is believed that the life forms that exist close to the core-mantle boundary, most likely around hydrothermal vents, would be less effected by the presence of humans on the surface.

So, to conclude, any act of terraforming these moons would invariably threaten any life form that already exists there. However, regardless of these facts, I hope I have convinced you all that terraforming these moons is something that Mankind needs to accomplish. Just picture it, huge floating indoor cities teeming with human life. Man has always dreamed of conquering the stars and my vision is one... terraform, let's colonize our solar-system and beyond. Let's journey deeper into the universe for we are the consciousness of the universe..."

Chapter 2

'Time passed... Everyone knows the name of the Great Professor Dabrowski. In the six hundred years since he convinced an earthbound committee that his theories were viable, mankind has fully escaped Earth's atmosphere and spread through the solar system like ants. His wonderful, glorious vision not only paved the way for terraformation but set in motion a scientific revolution which resulted in new robotics, spaceflight and longevity technologies. Today, on the anniversary of the terraforming committee's historic decision, we pay honour to Dr Dabrowski, without whom Ganymede, Europa and Callisto would not be terraformed, colonised and thriving with human settlement as they are today. These three water satellites are, of course, now known as the Golden Moons of Jupiter...'

Inside his work office at ISON - M.B, marine biologist Dr. Dvorak Duval switched off the vid screen which was replaying the celebrations of Dabrowski Day. He felt a little twinge of jealousy at the knowledge that his work would probably never be feted in the same way as Dabrowski's but he comforted himself with the thought that science was essentially a set of building blocks and that great discoveries were a combination of serendipity and all the smaller but no less important discoveries that came before.

"And if I am to make any discoveries at all," he chided himself, "I had better put some work in."

He focused on his computer screen, studying satellite images of colonised Europa. Information was flowing back in a constant stream. The floating cities fascinated him. Alien marine life had been discovered and as a marine biologist this gripped him with fascination. He would soon be there researching, exploring the Europan sea. The thought excited him. Visions of what lay ahead swam and flashed through his mind. He would make the long journey in a week's time. But the journey would seem timeless, non-existent as far as he was concerned. What he knew as reality would cease for a season as he underwent hibernation, cryogenics. He would be 'asleep' the entire journey, dwindling between semi-life and semi-death, kept alive... just. His thoughts turned to the weak gravity on Europa and how he would adjust to it. Studies in molecular biology showed that gravity and environment are key to the way man develops biologically.

The office door slid open, shaking him from his reverie. As usual, R-3, one of the many robot cooks, stepped into the room and walked over mechanically, ready to take a breakfast order. A cold clipped formality.

"Morning Dr Duval," it said with a smooth, male, humanoid voice, raising its fingeroid hand in greeting, refined algorithms working away efficiently, mathematically. "Would you like breakfast? The menu today is as follows..."

Dvorak promptly interjected... "Nothing today, R-3. Thanks..."

The robot turned and made its way out silently... ISON-M.B had thousands of these robot workers on site, working within different capacities. Some cooks or security guards and some aiding in complex scientific oceanic research in the Pacific and Atlantic, assisting and working alongside humans. Many had been sent out to the Golden Moons during the early days of terraforming when the initial stages were harsh and extreme and not many humans were prepared to sacrifice themselves. The human body is so delicate, not easy for it to adapt to such hostile worlds without there being biological changes and genetic mutations which could ultimately prove fatal. The long-term physiological effects on a human were deadly. This was of course still a problem, one which man tried his best to control and regulate.

Again, the door slid open and Dvorak sighed, despairing of ever settling down to work. This time a young man with dark brown hair and sharp crystal blue eyes walked in, his silver-coloured suit hanging neatly and elegantly from his lean athletic frame. The strong scent of his cologne tickled Dvorak's nostrils.

"Good morning, Dvorak... Thought I'd pop in for a minute..."

Dvorak looked up... "Greetings Alexander, sure come on in..."

Alexander walked over to a chair and sat, fiddling with the gold shining ring that encircled his plump white finger, the large finely polished oak desk standing between them.

"How are things going?"

"Great Alexander! In fact I've got some wonderful news."

"Let me guess you're heading out to the Jovian system, right?"

"Yes my friend and it's permanent."

"Congratulations Dvorak. Great news... Which moon?"

"They gave me the option of choosing any one of the three, I chose Europa."

Alexander leaned back on the flexi-chair and folded his arms. "Europa, hey... that's an average distance of 670,900 km from Jupiter. Man, I was looking at some old footage the other day, prior to terraforming. From a distance Europa seemed like nothing but a gigantic snowball, reflecting the light of the far-off Sun, a brilliant white. Much of its surface was covered with glittering hunks which looked like icebergs, formed from ammonia and water of course. Beautiful it was."

He paused momentarily...

"Then they showed some old footage of the atmospheric probes enclosed in heat shields, the ones that were gently nudged into orbit heading for Jupiter with the hope that they would survive long enough to send back some data before being crushed by Jupiter's immense gravitational force. The density of the gas around the probes steadily built up as they sank deeper into Jupiter's lost world... Those early days, eh..."

He rubbed his jaw reflectively, lost in thought for a brief moment as he pondered the images which shone bright in his mind.

"So, when was all this decided Dvorak? I mean your transfer out."

"Yesterday. The company directors here at ISON told me that they wanted to speak with me. We had a meeting, they made an offer, I accepted. ISON needs to send out as many of their best marine biologists as possible. Those ocean moons need us. So much research is going into exploring the ocean depths on each of the three moons."

"When are you leaving?"

"In a week's time... Can't wait! I've got nothing holding me back here, no wife, no family and limited friends. I'll be placed in one of the submarine Cities. I know that the large radiation shields, the ones in orbit, work very effectively. However there's even more protection from the radiation undersea. The submarine cities are massive and well concealed."

"What about the trip to the Jovian System itself? Can you deal with cryogenics?"

"Hibernation-related technologies have always fascinated me. No, the prospect of having to be frozen for a certain period during my space flight doesn't bother me in the slightest. Not to mention that statistically it's never gone wrong."

Alexander smiled his eyes bright, distant, as if he was picturing the journey himself. Then he frowned and asked, "So how exactly are they going to do it, the cryogenics I mean?"

"I must say Alexander, it's really fascinating... They are going to open my chest surgically, access the major blood vessels of my heart, put me on an open circuit through a pump and a chiller system removing as much blood as they possibly can, replacing it with a cryoprotectant. Then they will replace as much body fluid as they can with it, so there's no ice formation, no ice damage and once they have completely cryoprotected the cells, they'll drop the temperature to minus 90 degrees C. I could stay safely frozen for decades. And once I come out of my cryogenic state I'll be as healthy as ever. To my mind it certainly beats 'Galactic Consciousness Transfer' that's for sure." He smirked in amusement. "Sending consciousness across the galaxy, to solve the problem of physical galactic space travel... man that was something..."

"Yeah, it was only in operation for six months before it was shut down by the government, outlawed for obvious reasons. The main issue was when transferring the consciousness from one person to another, the transferred consciousness overwrote the consciousness of the receiving person. The moral and ethical implications were vast, which is why they stopped it."

He coughed into his hand and sat back, his eyes catching rays of sunlight.

"What about you Alexander, wouldn't you like a permanent transfer to... say Europa, or Ganymede? You are a good marine biologist yourself, one of the best here at ISON."

"Yes, it's the ultimate journey to go beyond the horizon of space. But I have commitments here and Earth's oceans will be plenty big enough for me, especially with you gone," he joked.

Dvorak's eyes now strayed towards his computer where satellite images of Europa continued to roll. He said, "The

Golden Moons, the submarine cities and the floating settlements that encircle those three satellites represent years of scientific research, engineering, mathematics. Mind is indeed a power in the universe my friend." He turned away from the screen gazing at Alexander, his eyes intense, philosophical...

"No question." He paused and with a finger scratched the tip of his nose...

"Ganymede was the one that always fascinated me from when I was a kid. Even the name itself demands scientific respect. Out of the three, that would be my pick. A moon that's even larger than Mercury, with a gravitational force of 1.428 m/s2 which is comparable to Earth's Moon... well, enough jaw, Dvorak, I better get back to my office. I'm pleased for you, my friend. We'll speak later?"

"Indeed we will my friend."

Both men stood up and shook hands as beams of sunlight filtered into the room.

Alexander turned and made his way out, his steps fading into silence. Dvorak sat back down, his eyes instantly fixed back on the screen where a massive underwater bubble-shaped structure came into view, one of the many submarine cities where he would soon be living. Then the thought of leaving behind majestic Earth forever hit him.

The great parks of green, the blue sky, the cities, the seasons, the winds and rain, the desert sands, the mountains which stretched on forever, the jungles rich with flora and fauna, the rigging of the boats in harbour, the fresh morning air, the avenue of trees and the moss-grown gardens, the animals, the insects, it all would become nothing but beautiful memories stored within the very depths of his mind... He stood up and walked to the window and gazed at the Sun. Its light was glorious. It blazed with an ancient magnificence. That too would be missed. He stood there transfixed, almost hypnotized, his eyes fixed towards the blue sky of Earth and beyond...

"I've been living in this submarine city on Europa for five years now and it never gets tiring," thought Dr Dvorak Duval, slightly dazzled by the powerful overhead lights that flooded the indoor world. He walked carefully through the city centre with the strange gait adopted by all the inhabitants, on his way to work. He still had not quite adjusted to the low gravity but the problem remained the same for all who were encapsulated under the sea of this alien world and for those above who lived on the surface on the floating cities. On Europa, the human body had to learn a whole new set of reflexes. It had for the first time to distinguish between mass and weight.

Dressed in his milky turquoise work uniform which all the scientists within his division wore, he brushed past the crowds. Tides of people moved around, adults, children, scattered everywhere, going about their day. The persistent buzz of noise bothered him. For a moment one could be fooled into believing that they were on Earth. The shops, the lights, even the pseudo-floral scent filling the air, all conspired to give the impression that one was merely walking through an indoor shopping centre on Earth. But the low gravity and the thick glass which encircled the huge steel bubble structure separating man from sea was a constant reminder to all that this was indeed another world.

A large bright screen hung in one corner showing some very old, interesting historical space footage: the early days of space exploration. The images rolled... Dvorak stopped walking and stood watching for a moment as a lunar carrier pulled away with ease from a Space Station, low-thrust plasma jets blasting their electrified streams into space. The ship was no longer bound to planet Earth. The umbilical cord had been severed breaking the bonds of gravity. Next, images of the ship, the lunar carrier appeared across the screen in the final stages of descent. A Moon landing. The descending ship was poised almost above the line dividing night from day. Directly below was a chaos of jagged shadows and dazzling isolated peaks catching the first light of the lunar dawn. Then the ship started to drift slowly towards the night side of the Moon which was not completely dark. It was aglow with a seemingly ghostly light. Planet Earth, its gigantic neighbor was flooding the barren land below with its glorious radiance. Dvorak smiled. He had been to Luna once before, a leisurely vacation, his first real space adventure. The images brought back many vivid memories of his short time there and led him to make a brief calculation. 'A person who weighed 180 pounds on Earth would only weigh 30 pounds on the Moon... If you moved in a straight line at a uniform speed you felt a fantastic sense of buoyancy...'

The screen was displaying images of the lunar landscape. It was peppered with towering mountain peaks and craters that could swallow up cities and the shuttle, via automatic controls, was steadily falling towards its landing site. The jets gave one final spurt causing the shuttle to rock a little. Then it finally made contact with the barren world of Luna. He noticed a group of robot workers standing beneath the screen, metallic and bright, appearing to watch the scenes above. They seemed taken in by the historical event as they began to converse amongst themselves. Dvorak moved on swiftly, letting his memories of his time on the Moon slip away. It was time to refocus, get to work and continue his oceanic research here on Jupiter's watery moon of Europa.

Within a short while he arrived at his working quarters. Time didn't seem to exist on Europa, and he had almost lost his sense of it, especially living in the indoor world, deep beneath the Europan Sea. Not to mention that day and night as he had remembered it on Earth were no more. The huge structure itself was held up by long steel pillars that met with the ocean floor. The Europan sea was peppered with many of these structures which housed thousands of people; giant indoor cities. Entering his private office, he could hear the all too familiar sound of hissing as oxygen was perpetually pumped into the room. Through the thick glass, a variety of marine life was visible. Dvorak stood for a moment, as he had done countless times since his transfer, gazing out at the ocean beasts as they moved gracefully, almost symbiotically. This was what he lived for. It was as if he could almost touch them. Symbiotic life of all kinds, shapes and sizes thrived in the warm waters. Then he caught sight of something that looked like a jellyfish, it was transparent, glowing, pulsating with vivid alternating colours; bioluminescence.

As he approached his large white rectangular desk, he fell into his chair, a low gravity fall. He switched on the computer and the monitor flashed into life. To his right a large control panel gleamed. Lights flashed above radar screens. Numbers came and went across computer displays. Then a news bulletin flashed. It caught his attention... 'The Golden Moons Conference coming soon.' It was a political gathering imposed by the leaders of Earth, nothing more.

His mind started to work and he ran through what he knew about the mystical Gas Giant, Jupiter and the affinity it had with Europa and indeed with the other moons. Europa orbited the Gas Giant Jupiter every 3.5 days and was tidally-locked, locked by gravity to the Gas Giant so the same hemisphere of the moon always faced the planet. Dvorak contemplated this affinity between the two. It took the Gas Giant 4,333 Earth days, around 12 Earth years, to orbit the sun... a Jovian year. Jupiter's equator and the orbital plane of its moons were tilted with respect to Jupiter's orbital path around the Sun by only 3 degrees. This meant that Jupiter spun nearly upright so that the planet, as well as Europa and Jupiter's other moons, did not have extreme seasons as other planets did.

These thoughts were soon shattered by the buzzing sound coming from the intercom unit across his desk. It emitted a piercing electronic shriek, like a distorted time signal. The screen lit up and a face appeared in ripples of visual static.

"Dvorak, how are you? How's the research going my friend?"

"Hey Marcel, I'm good... We are discovering new sea creatures practically every other day. In fact, we have found a creature that resembles the medusas found in the seas of Earth. It has trailing tentacles that are armed with stinging cells. It's complex looking alright... Who knows what else we will discover in this vast mysterious Europan sea-world?"

"For sure," replied Marcel as the waves of visual static continued to dance across the screen. "Anyhow, are we still meeting later? Meal's on me remember..."

"I'll let you know my friend..."

"Okay... but don't keep me waiting too long."

Marcel winked and the screen across the intercom faded to black. All sound died. Dvorak leaned back and rubbed his eyes. There was much to do, much to consider. As a marine biologist he was part of a team of scientists that were focused on discovering all that lay in the Europan Sea. Then he heard the sound of rushing feet, a flow of energy. He stood up. One of his colleagues, Dr Bruce White rushed in, and from the expression on his face and the glare in his deep-set eyes, he had news to break.

"Dvorak, you won't believe this... We have just discovered something that will change the course of history..." He paused for breath, staring hard. "We have recovered the body of a robot, yes, a machine, AI, found floating in the ocean just above our submarine city... and it's not one of ours."

Dvorak's eyes grew wide in wonder. He was hit with a sense of irony. He would never have expected this. Regardless he understood the immense implications.

He said, "When was it recovered?"

"About two hours ago... Earth hours that is."

"Where is it now?"

"The two divers responsible for finding the robot brought it here into the marine biology department. It's in our work quarters, room E."

"Is it operative, functioning?"

"It took a bit of time, but it is now. Come... quick."

A few minutes later, Dvorak and Bruce stepped into room E. A tall metallic gold-coloured robot sat on a bed, its photocell eyes shining and in the bright light of the room the complex-looking machine looked menacing. It had large fingeroid hands and long powerful metallic legs. Sadly, the robot had been corrupted mercilessly by the Europan Sea but it still seemed to function well, at least partially. Sitting beside it was marine biologist Dr Zubrin, his green eyes wide with awe.

"I've been trying to communicate with it. Nothing so far..." he muttered.

Dvorak and Bruce stood there gazing at the machine in amazement, mouths agape as they focused on the gleaming mass. It was unlike the robots that man had built. This robot was distinctly different to any man-made machine, so what was it doing there? From where had it come? How long had it been there? Who or what was responsible for building such a machine? All three were filled with a burning curiosity. Dvorak and Bruce each positioned a chair in close proximity to the machine and sat. Dvorak licked his lips pensively and said, targeting the question at Zubrin, "So you haven't communicated with it at all?"

"No, nothing yet..."

Dvorak rubbed his head thoughtfully. "Well give it more time, it's obviously damaged. One thing for sure, it is an absolute miracle that you managed to get it working again, especially after finding it floating in the ocean depths."

"The fact that it is operating again, with restored robotic consciousness has nothing to do with me or anyone here Dvorak," muttered Zubrin emphatically. "We just dried it down, laid it on the bed... ran a few tests, and that was it. We were just hopeful. Then, to our amazement, robotic consciousness was suddenly restored, defying all odds. The first forty-five minutes it was seemingly lifeless, inoperative.

After that it suddenly opened its photocell eyes, started to move, gazed around, and sat up."

The swift buzz from Zubrin's intercom speaker broke the flow. A husky yet controlled masculine voice spoke. "Zubrin, the AI team are on their way. They should be there soon."

"Okay, thank you..."

Seconds of weighted silence passed, hearts beating hard, fast, tension building. Then suddenly the machine spoke for the first time since its rescue. "I'm X-10..." Its humanoid voice was hard yet refined.

Zubrin, completely overwhelmed, battling to compose himself, gasped superfluously, "Look, it's speaking..."

All eyes were focused, locked onto the machine.

Again, it spoke, "My mission has one purpose. To reach Europa, and deliver a message, one that will change the face of human history."

It went silent, still. All three men gazed at each other with glazed eyes, as if under the influence of some kind of magical hypnosis that had taken hold of their souls, their minds. They refocused, looking at the machine. The robot got slowly to its feet and walked to the corner of the room, its gold frame standing out distinctly against the cold pale walls. It was obvious to all that it had sustained some internal damage. It turned and focused on the startled men and then spoke...

"As I entered the Europan atmosphere I prepared to land my ship on one of the huge floating settlements that my navigation system had mapped out. But due to a technical malfunction, my ship went down crashing into the ocean. I was left at the mercy of the Europan Sea."

"When did this all happen?" asked Dvorak, curious eyes burning like fire.

"Chronologically," it paused as memory banks clicked. "I crashed my ship seven Earth hours ago..."

"Who sent you exactly?" Bruce snapped.

"Our makers, an elite alien race... They are known as the Valagats. They look very humanoid in appearance, slightly bigger heads and eyes, which gives them amazingly enhanced vision. They have decided that now is the time to deliver the message to the human-race. Their planet, Volkan, is situated in another region of the galaxy, the Milky Way, twenty-one thousand light years from Earth. We super-machines have learnt to live in harmony with our makers, the Valagats. The planet Volkan is beautiful, almost the same size as Earth in terms of mass, in fact, it is almost an identical copy of your planet, slightly smaller, but it is filled with jungles, forests, lakes, mountains, flora, fauna, animals of all kinds. The similarities between Earth and Volkan are simply incredible. However, unlike Earth, Volkan has more land than sea. Seventy percent of the planet is land, the other thirty, sea."

Dvorak turned swiftly to Zubrin not wanting to interrupt and whispered in his left ear, "Seems to know so much about our planet, Earth. I wonder how?"

The robot picked up on this, however.

"Through special probes and satellite-systems the Valagats obtained colossal amounts of information pertaining to Earth. These probes were sent into deep space and gave the Valagats all the necessary information and data they needed concerning Earth, including images of the landscape. Earth is indeed beautiful and its people have achieved so much throughout the passage of time. The human mind is complex, brilliant, and capable of the unimaginable. But the moons of Jupiter were best left alone. You should not have come..."

Zubrin stood up, his white face reflecting the sense of icy dread which swept through all three men, but his features quickly reddened as a burning anger rushed in and took control. He said, "What the hell are you talking about?"

The robot replied, "The three Golden Moons, as you call them, belong to the Valagats, my masters. A century before man set foot here in the Jovian system, the Valagats had already landed and explored these moons making preparations to terraform. They never anticipated human invasion. You should not have come."

Dvorak got to his feet, adrenaline surging through his system. "Look here," he snapped. "It all comes down to this... We humans did the job first. We came, terraformed, colonised and have taken control of the three Golden Moons. Through science, engineering and technology Man has conquered the Jovian system. Europa, Ganymede and Callisto now belong to us, my kind. We are the authority here."

Again the robot replied, "I can only reemphasize my initial point... A century before man set foot here in the Jovian system, the Valagats had already landed and explored these moons making preparation for a Jovian takeover."

Composing himself, Dvorak replied, "If these aliens came here a century before man set foot on these moons, why did they not act and start the terraforming process back then? Why wait so long? This all seems a little odd and perhaps inconsistent."

"The reason is simple. The Valagats work systematically, that is, they have been terraforming other moons and planets within their solar-system, and other systems that are relatively close. It is all a question of priority based on distance and timing."

"Yes, but the fact remains that we humans beat them to it," argued Dvorak... "Unfortunately for them, Man went on to terraform these moons ahead of them and we colonised them. There is no need to terraform anymore because it has already been done by human hand, nor is there any place for your Valagats on the Golden Moons because Man has made them home."

The robot's next words hit like raging thunder, "All humans must leave the Golden Moons and return back to Earth at once, a mass human exodus of Europa, Ganymede and Callisto. The Golden Moons belong to the Valagats. If you refuse the consequences will be devastating. This is the message I had to deliver. Please comply."

"This is piracy," blasted Zubrin, his face almost purple with anger. "Why should we leave and give these aliens our terraformed Moons? These Valagats are nothing but alien pirates. We terraformed, colonised and claim the Golden Moons as ours. The fact that the Valagats visited here a century before is irrelevant. They did nothing after. What matters is that human beings have terraformed these moons and made them home. Human beings put in the work, the finance, the research, the technology, the time and now a bunch of aliens want to come along and usurp it all. No way!

"Absolutely," cried Bruce, fists clenched, eyes burning with fury.

Dvorak intervened. "The Golden Moons of Jupiter belong to the human race. Tell that to your alien masters, these pirates. We are here to stay."

"That is your last word?"

"Absolutely," replied Dvorak. You can speak to any of our leaders, anyone on Earth or Mars or Luna or The Golden Moons themselves. They would all say the same."

Robot X-10 lowered its head in silent farewell... With a lightning flip of its hand, it touched a switch which was positioned neatly across its chest. Everything went black... All sound and light was consumed by this intense blackness that swirled and swirled and swirled. The three men grabbed at each other trying to steady themselves before they were vaporised out of existence. The power of the blast was such that it caused a devastating ripple effect that could be felt on the surface. And it would not end there.

The Valagats would soon come...but the war had already begun.

Ultimate Robot

Leopold Malinski sat in silence. He was dressed in his white spacesuit, helmet put to one side, as he gazed through the small circular window of his cabin on Ganymede, contemplating the alien world before him. Dark regions of the landscape were saturated with impact craters, lighter regions, crosscut by extensive grooves and ridges. The Jovian system was certainly one to behold. Shuttling back and forth in the equatorial plane were the dazzling moons of Callisto, Europa, Io, and of course, Ganymede itself, orbiting satellites of the grand master Jupiter.

Ganymede was tidally locked, one side always facing toward the planet, and that was the side he was on now, safely sealed away in his small cabin fed with a breathable atmosphere. The ever-present pest that was the great Gas Giant Jupiter, a sphere of shifting turbulent clouds, constantly blasting out charged particles which would circle the planet like the Van Allen Belts of Earth, was large in the sky emitting its radiation. However, much of that radiation was deflected away from this moon, due to the large radiation shields in orbit.

Jupiter was indeed a mysterious planet to all who viewed it from Ganymede; an enigma to say the least and one that Leopold would ever marvel at. Because the moon's rotation period was synchronous with its orbit it meant that from any point on Ganymede's surface, Jupiter always remained in the same position in the sky. So, on the near-side of Ganymede where Leopold was stationed, the great Gas Giant was always visible, whilst it could never be seen from the far-side of its satellite. The beauty of the cloud bands and even the transits of the inner moons crossing its surface were always on show from this position but Leopold had found that Ganymede's orbit of Jupiter had another rather spectacular feature. When this moon crossed the sunny side of the planet, Jupiter would appear as a fully lit disc but as it traversed towards the shadow side, the gas giant would appear to be gradually shrinking to a thin crescent which would balloon again as the moon returned to the sunny side. That man's inventiveness, creativity and sheer genius had allowed him to witness this was almost beyond contemplation.

He yawned and rubbed his head, tearing his gaze away from the celestial splendour. He could hear the throbbing of pumps as precious oxygen was pumped into the cabin but thin traces of gas would sometimes escape, rushing out into space and the atmosphere was getting a little foul as the purifiers worked away, battling to take control. He sighed. A day had finally passed on Ganymede, but a day was a long pull here, nothing like a swift Earth-day, chronologically speaking. It took this moon just over seven earth days to complete one orbit of Jupiter so in effect, a day on Ganymede was equivalent to just over a week back on Earth. But, the sun still rose and the sun still set, even if it was over the very long Ganymede day. Leopold had been interested to discover that due to Ganymede's very small axial tilt, the sun rose almost due east and set almost due west no matter where you were on the surface. This could be observed from both sides but only on this side could you witness Jupiter change its phase.

He had been here for some time, accompanied by thirty other scientists and a team of robots. Each member of the team had their own quarters where they could cook, wash and entertain themselves, mostly by reading books. Work-computers could also be used as a form of entertainment. But once they left their cabin, reality hit. Oxygen masks had to be deployed. And getting used to the weak gravity was also a challenge. As for the robots, a total of sixty, they all remained together, stationed in a large air-locked dome where the scientists would meet and plan accordingly. The mission was simple: explore and take geological samples with the aim to terraform.

Leopold could see the other cabins from his window. They were close by, all neatly positioned. It gave him a sense of peace and tranquillity, reminding him that in his temporary solitude, he was not alone. Every few minutes, the radar transmitter would gather its strength and send out a silent thunderclap of power. No echoes of new satellites came pulsing back. It had been well established, Jupiter had seventy-nine moons and that was that. He swallowed hard and his thoughts turned to his dream of terraforming Ganymede. How incredible it would be to stand out in the open and watch Jupiter change its phase, unhampered by the tiny window through which he viewed it now.

The inevitable difficulties that were to come drifted around in his head like the tangled orbits of the asteroids. He reached over to the small table beside him and picked up a tube of chocolate flavoured paste. It had all the essential vitamins and minerals one would need. Opening the tube, he placed it in his mouth and pressed. The paste coursed down his throat, giving him renewed energy... He smiled wryly as he remembered how he had hated them at the beginning of his mission and how he barely thought about it after the first couple of days. Who had time to worry about taste on a voyage traversing millions of miles of space, with the fear of asteroid collision and the demands of the vision screens and the instrumentation of the control deck?

It had not all been action of course. There were long periods when the centrifuge turned slowly on its axis, generating its imitation gravity as he and the other astronauts slept in their cubicles whilst the ship pierced the emptiness of space. But some images were bright in his mind like the time he realised they were only two hours away from Jupiter. He had checked and rechecked the ship's orbit with great care and focus. The calculations suggested that there was no need for further speed corrections until the moment of closest approach. The adrenaline rush he experienced as they got closer to the Gas Giant was like nothing he had felt before; a great spasm of hope and fear. Minute by minute it grew bigger and the thought of being dragged down to destruction by the planet's immense gravitational field had played on his mind during those moments. But they were moving too swiftly for even Jupiter's gravity to capture them.

Then there was the time when the ship went into a near-grazing orbit, just enough to miss the atmosphere by a few hundred miles. Jupiter filled the sky; it was immense, hard to fathom when viewed by the human eye. The colours were majestic, yellows, pinks, reds. He smiled with pride that he was one of the first to see it so closely and this stimulated another memory of the time when the ship's orbit was diving into the shadow of Jupiter, soon to pass over the night side of the immense planet. The giant nuclear reactor that is the Sun, was sinking quickly into the Jovian clouds, its rays spreading out along the horizon before it contracted and died in a majestic blaze of chromatic glory...

His thoughts drifted to the many probes that had been launched, probes that would make contact with Jupiter's atmosphere, giving Man a minor glimpse of that mysterious world. Some would never be heard from again, burned up before they could send out any information. Others would slice through the upper layers of the Jovian atmosphere then glide out once more into outer space. Jupiter's atmospheric composition, temperature, magnetic fields, and radioactivity were awe-inspiring. It was an immense ball of gas and liquid, its mass 2.5 times that of all the other planets in the Solar System combined; an atmosphere that contained trace amounts of methane, water vapour, ammonia, and silicon-based compounds, with fractional amounts of carbon, phosphine, neon, oxygen, ethane, and hydrogen sulfide.

The probes relayed images of alien scenes and shapes and vivid colours as they fell through the brutal turbulent atmosphere of yellowish, golden mist. The mist at one point disappeared as the probes fell through the base of a high layer of cloud and emerged into a clear region, a region of almost pure hydrogen. One of the probes twisted around in the thickening atmosphere, presumably as a result of some sudden turbulence. Eventually, all the probes would be swallowed up by the Gas Giant as they fell deeper into its mysterious atmosphere, the density of gas around them building in intensity, the pressure mounting. Under the weight of miles and miles of turbulent atmosphere and immense gravitational forces, nothing could survive for long.

He needed rest. Still dressed, he stretched out on his bunk. For some reason a memory of sitting inside the ship thinking deeply about Alpha Centauri, a gravitationally bound system of the closest stars and exoplanets to the Solar System at 4.37 light years from the sun drifted into his consciousness. He dismissed that thought along with its questions and possibilities that would keep him awake for hours more and instead bought up a memory of listening to all the systems functioning, working away within the ship as they should as he sat on the Control Deck, floating amongst the stars, the centrifuge turning slowly on its axis, generating its imitation gravity. It was relaxing and somewhat mesmeric. As he finally drifted towards sleep, he felt a deep satisfaction in the fact that all his powers and skills had been directed to one end, Ganymede. Human space evolution was driving towards new goals and he was part of it, part of the engine that would make it happen.

Time stretched and Leopold was once again sitting alone in his private office in the oxygen-pumped dome. A centrifugal force produced an artificial gravity within the dome and happily, this was enough to prevent physical atrophy. Outside radiation detectors noted and analysed incoming cosmic rays from the Galaxy. Neutron and X-ray telescopes kept watch on stars that no human eye would see. Scratching his hard jaw, he contemplated the scientific data pertaining to terraforming as it presented itself to him across the computer screen, the hazy white light casting shadows across his hard-lined face. The fulfilment of his assigned project, which was to Terraform, was more than an obsession; it was the only reason for his existence. He prowled over the data endlessly, the diagrams, the physics, the science, undistracted by the passions and lusts of organic life. Across from him on the wall was a TV screen where programmes played, beamed to Ganymede from Earth. The current programme was about deep-space probes; probes of the last half-century, and how they often reached planets, but then failed to send back any data, any information because their antennas couldn't locate Earth.

Then the familiar view of Earth appeared on the screen. Leopold's eyes lit up; how he missed it, but there was much work to do. He watched the view of majestic Earth, now waxing past the half-moon phase as it gloriously swept towards the far side of the Sun then turned back to his data.

A little while later, a robot stepped into the room, tall and silver. This was no ordinary robot; it stood out from the rest, in that, this machine housed a human consciousness, the consciousness of Burt Kennedy. It was actually a walking avatar. Of course, the real Burt Kennedy was dead, physically speaking, but his personality, his mind lived on within this machine. This was known as digital immortality, brain uploading. The creation of this digital avatar by an artificial intelligence platform that analysed personal data and correspondence meant that Burt Kennedy lived on. Machine-learning algorithms were responsible for this, performing brainwave-pattern scanning, then producing a digital copy. The machine spoke just like the deceased in question, retaining all memory and intellectual capacity. Paradoxically Burt was dead yet alive. Philosophically this became a complex metaphysical tangle that led to much debate amongst the great thinkers of the time in terms of what consciousness really is. Burt, the man who had died decades ago, was one of the first men to have flown into space, a top astronaut; a pioneer of his time and this was the reason why his mind and personality had been preserved, uploaded into this working avatar, a machine.

"Come in," said Leopold as if talking to a human. To him the external part, the robot, became nothing but an unimportant blur. Leopold saw in it the astronaut and scientist Burt Kennedy.

Burt walked over to the desk and sat facing him. It disconnected from its robotic function and became pure mind. It, or him depending on one's perspective said, "Leopold, it's not going to be easy to terraform Ganymede, to create a planetary biosphere that mimics Earth. It will be a challenge."

"Have faith... we will accomplish the seemingly impossible Burt. Once we terraform Ganymede, it will result in the creation of an ocean world. There's water under the surface; a saltwater ocean estimated at a drilling depth of 200km."

Leopold sat back, his eyes wide with enthusiasm. "Isn't it amazing what we have achieved thus far through technology? We are so very close Burt... We will override all the potential problems that may arise and terraform. We will make history..."

"Yes Leopold... If Man has come this far it is all to do with that innate hunger within the soul of Man, that burning desire to conquer the stars. That hunger and drive has catapulted Man forward to this point. Man has this instinct to explore, to take risks and bring about change..."

For a brief moment, they sat in silence. Then Burt folded its arms and continued...

"Since the dawn of time, the universe has fascinated even the ancient eye. Even early man, ape-man, in the harsh logic of survival, would have surely been fascinated by space, naive hands reaching out to touch the ghostly face of the moon as it rose slowly amid equatorial constellations. And now, through the passage of time the barriers of distance between astronomical bodies have crumbled thanks to incredible advancements in both science and engineering. Man finally built a machine that would grace the heavens, space itself, and venture into the very depths of the Universe..."

"Yes Burt, and now we are so close to conquering the stars themselves," said Leopold, wondering where his friend was heading with this.

"Yes indeed, and it happened during my lifetime as a human being. I was one of those that wanted to conquer the stars myself. That's why I became one of the first astronauts, scientists, a pioneer if you like, to enter space. In this context, let me briefly recount to you my experience, my first journey into the void, my unique experience, the early days of spaceflight, and that moment when I reached Space Station 1. A life changing moment in more ways than you can imagine. Now I know that you might deem this as pointless, pointless information given that you are a highly experienced astronaut yourself, but it's the past that shapes the present. History is so vitally important, and I'm a piece of history that lives on in a machine. So, indulge me..."

Leopold spread his hands in a gesture of acquiescence, crossed his legs and sat with a hand on his chin. This would be interesting.

"My biggest battle was in the mind, as it is for most. Once in the spacecraft, I settled into the seat, adjusting the safety harness around my waist and shoulders. I was so focused that it seemed as if I was alone. The other crew members became almost ghostly figures... Then, almost immediately, I became sharply aware of the colossal forces coiled around me. The energy of a nuclear bomb would be used to blow me out into space a mere two hundred miles from Earth; a fantastically controlled explosion. Then the fiery roar of the rockets came, the pressure of acceleration. Then lift off...

Finally, I was heading towards space, the heavens beyond, my blood racing through my body with force, mouth dry. When acceleration came on again, as the upper-stage rockets fired, the thrust was much gentler... softer. Then, eventually dawn exploded outside the ship. We were shooting through veils of crimson, blue and pink into the white of day. Even through the heavily tinted windows, which were there in order to reduce the glare, beams of sunlight swept in across the cabin, and to me, it was almost a spiritual encounter. Then as time elapsed, space, utter darkness engulfed the ship as it eased itself into orbit. The thunder of the engines gradually dropped, until they died... There was total silence. At this point the only thing that prevented me from floating were the restraining straps. I remember I was hit by a sense of no-time, as if the immensity of time no longer existed and had been swallowed up. Shortly after I caught a glimpse of the Atlantic Ocean, two hundred miles below, and from space it was indeed a spectacle, the glare of Earth filling half the sky. Then Space Station 1 came into view, slowly revolving once a minute, the centrifugal force generated by this slow spin producing an artificial gravity equal to the Moon's... the Earth's Moon, of course. It gave Moon-bound passengers a chance to become acclimatised. As we approached, I could see the central axis of the Space Station, with its docking arms. Eventually with the softest of thuds, ship and station made contact. I recall hearing those metallic scratching noises from outside. And then of course the brief hissing of air as the pressures equalised. Then the Station orbited towards the night side of the planet, planet Earth..."

Leopold noted with interest that there was now something in its gaze that went beyond the capacity of any robot, a dawning awareness. But this was no surprise really. After all, this machine housed the consciousness of Burt Kennedy. It said...

"Leopold I'm going to end my brief encounter with spaceflight here and move to my next point. This experience had a monumental effect on me. That whole experience dramatically changed me. That brief journey into space. As a result, I started to think about life from a more spiritual perspective. I had been a borderline atheist, but that soon changed."

Leopold was interested in what the avatar had to say but time was ticking and the data and analyses on the screens behind him were calling.

"Okay Burt, I get how that might be but...can you get to the point?"

"Well, the one thing that rolled around in my mind after that spaceflight was this... What gave Man the intellectual capacity to achieve such wonders? What was responsible for giving Man that innate knowledge that led them to reach space and accomplish amazing feats? Epistemology, what is knowledge and from where does it fundamentally come was a question that I carried around with me after that spaceflight to Space Station 1."

"I see," said Leopold in a calm low voice his attention returning fully to his companion. Although working through a robot, an avatar, Burt was as human as could be. This impressed Leopold greatly. Transhumanism working at its finest... he thought. Burt continued...

"Leopold, we can sit here for decades to come talking about the greatness of man, and all the inventions that have come to pass which inevitably led to Spaceflight, and all the other mind-shattering discoveries that have changed the face of human history. All those brilliant minds of the past like, Archimedes, Socrates, Plato, Leonardo da Vinci, Niels Bohr, Max Planck, Erwin Schrodinger, Werner Heisenberg, Einstein, Dirac and many, many others that have come and gone throughout the course of time. But again, the question remains... what was, or is, responsible for implanting that seed of knowledge into the human soul? The human mind is something to behold, it's a force, a power that changes and creates new realities. The human mind is so complex, convoluted and brilliant. The quantum mechanics, the sub-atomic interplay within the brain, the human soul, intelligence, consciousness and so forth, is something that can't really be explained and is all interconnected to something greater."

"What are you suggesting Burt?"

"An infinite being... There must be something that propels Man forward intellectually and controls the mechanisms of consciousness... the mind, the soul. This could only be a creator, eternal in nature. Yes, experience, existence, leads to knowledge, understanding and so forth, the development of one's conscious experience of reality, but that only explains things to a certain point. In other words, there must be something that transcends Man, something that is at the centre point of all knowledge, from where all knowledge flows, and it is this infinite being that dwells beyond time and space. Only an infinite being could be the fountain from where all knowledge flows and is given to Man in various proportions."

There was a brief pause as the robot contemplated...

"My conclusion is this... epistemology has to be housed in some kind of theology. If one takes an atheistic approach, then all the brilliance and knowledge that comes from Man is ultimately meaningless and will fade and return into the void from where it had initially come. Yes, all knowledge, consciousness, has to be connected to theology... Thus, there must be a maker, a creator, an infinite being that holds all of the mechanisms of life together, including consciousness and knowledge... Now think about this... we are all here on a terraforming project, man and machine. And we are all hopeful we will succeed. But have you ever asked yourself this question? Who was responsible for the planetary engineering of Earth... its atmosphere, temperature, and so forth? Humans take this for granted. But they need to think about it. As far as I'm concerned, whatever it was has to be the greatest mind of all.

Ganymede was eventually terraformed. An ocean world of floating settlements had been established. Leopold who had been heavily influenced by the philosophical and theological thoughts of Burt Kennedy named one of the settlements after him, Kennedy City...

Life Force

"SUICIDE...! It committed suicide," snapped detective Lacombe reading the note he had found beside the cold metallic body. A large gaping hole had been blown neatly into its chest-cavity via the aid of a powerful handgun. A maze of intricate wires blackened and torn by the blast were visible, semi-destroyed circuit boards and electrical components too... The handgun lay beside the machine.

The note read: 'Life is meaningless, thus I, X-7 have decided to terminate my life via the aid of a handgun...'

Lacombe placed the note into his long grey coat and muttered, "It caused its own death would you believe? This is the first case ever. Had this occurred six months ago we could have had it brought back to life, worked out what was going on but the new government law forbids this."

"Death?" snapped the police officer who stood beside him looking at the lifeless robot with a sickly kind of excitement. "I'm sorry Sir, but a robot can't die. It wasn't alive in the first place. Only humans, insects and animals die. A robot can only cease to operate."

Lacombe responded, "Well most people might see it that way Parker, but as far as I'm concerned, it was a living entity in its own right, that through the complexity of its system developed self-awareness, consciousness. Taking all those factors into consideration it was alive as far as I'm concerned. Those geniuses at ETSU Robotics are responsible for creating a new kind of being... a new kind of life force. The complexity of a mechanical mind is simply staggering, an ever-evolving robotic consciousness. The mathematics used in working out robotic brain-paths is so convoluted it's frightening. The neural networks that build new connections within a machine's mechanical brain is a form of neural plasticity which also occurs within human brain function. It's simply fantastic, mysterious to say the least."

Parker rubbed his sweaty forehead and said, "Are you suggesting that robots ultimately have a soul?"

"If a machine can think, regardless of how thought process is induced and rationally self-reflect on the past and evaluate consequences and weigh decisions accordingly, then yes, in a real sense it does. It's a life force of its own... You need to remember Parker that these robots are fully sentient, rational agents that can experience pain, pleasure, sadness, joy, mood change... Robots can be altruistic, others not so much. They can make decisions just like this robot here did, choosing to end its mechanical life. Machines are so evolved now that they even have a moral compass. In light of all this... yes, I think a machine is ultimately alive and does have a soul."

Lacombe walked over to the window and there he halted. The air was moist. He gazed out into the night darkness. The street below was bustling with sound and wild city activity. Surface-vehicles raced by and city lights flickered. People hurried around stepping in and out of shops, robots too. He then looked up at the cold orb of the Moon as it hung high suspended in the blackness of outer space. It glared terribly bright, casting an incredible complexity of lines and shadows. Stars shone with creative energy, vibrant and thrilling. He turned to face Parker, the large archaic clock ticking away in the corner...

"Detective Lacombe," snapped Parker, his face a manifestation of concern. "This may be the first case of a robot committing suicide but it might not be the last! Other suicides may follow. But what's most concerning is if a machine can 'kill itself,' it could in turn kill others... like a human being. The implications here are serious and vast Sir."

Lacombe nodded his head in acknowledgment, his cold blue eyes hard and stern as he reflected on this horrifying possibility. The same thought had leapt into his mind. Parker knelt beside the lifeless robot his eyes roaming in the cold light of the room. Beside the inert machine lay a newspaper, the New York Chronicle. On the front page in bold it read: 'Come visit the Golden Moons of Jupiter for a memory of a lifetime.' Beneath it, written untidily in black ink, the disturbed robot had written the words... 'Even my desire to visit the Golden Moons was ultimately an illusion.'

"Parker," said Lacombe sharply. "This is most worrying. So far, a robot has never committed murder, never killed a human being, not one incident. But as these machines evolve and become more and more human the probability of a robot killing someone randomly increases drastically. Remember evil only exists within the very soul of Man as an acting potential within the reptilian complex. Too much electrical and chemical activity within that region of the brain brings out the worst in Man, utter evil. So, on a parallel scale, what if machines, like humans, develop that same type of abnormality within their neural networks in their efforts to become more human and then go out and do evil acts? After all, what is it to be human? Sadly, for some, part of the human condition is to kill, take life. As these machines become more human, developing their own personalities and identities then yes, it's just a question of time before a killer machine strikes!"

From Under the Eye of a Machine

"Johnny," said his wife merrily, walking into the kitchen, warm sunlight streaming across her slim, chiselled face. "Have you heard about this new invention, quantum tunnelling? 'The Magical Belt,' is what they call it."

Johnny placed his warm mug of mint-coffee on the table and stretched as he battled the early morning drowsiness. He glanced up at her, and she smiled.

"Yes Sanny."

"You don't sound impressed?"

"It's pseudo-science, nonsense," he replied, his eyes straying towards the window from where the morning sunlight streamed into the room. "This so-called inventor claims that this belt allows you to walk through walls because it generates a field of energy through and around the person wearing it. Basically, this energy field will reduce the boundary energies restricting the subatomic particles in both the wall and person to their proper positions."

Sanny stood there sipping on her mug of tea.

"Lowering the boundary energies, the inherent wavelike quality of subatomic particles allows atoms to pass between each other. Sounds complex, almost believable, but it simply won't work..."

Sanny shrugged and switched on the small Tele-set... An advert flashed into life. Audio followed. 'Call The Adjustment Group, the one and only Transhumanist agency in the world licensed to make drastic brain alterations of cosmological proportions.'

Johnny's eyes widened and his gaze fixed on the tele-set. Sanny caught his expression, registering the implications that came with it. She abruptly shut down the tele-set, stepped towards the breakfast table and sat.

"You are still thinking about it, aren't you?" she accused, two dots of red forming across her cheeks. "You are as predictable as the law of gravity Johnny. Sweetheart I thought we had spoken about this?"

Resting his elbows on the table, he replied, "Sanny, I'm not going to lie to you, it's something that is always on my mind."

"Mind..." she scoffed. "Yes, mind being the operative word Johnny..." She paused momentarily, then snapped. "These people are brain butchers."

"Sanny, The Adjustment Group has been running for six months now, government approved... it's very safe and the science behind their technology is simply amazing."

"So what? You want to replace your brain with a mechanical one? Are you serious? You'll become nothing but an organic robot, don't you see that, Johnny?"

"It's not what you think Sanny and the list of advantages are endless... besides, it's relatively cheap. Most people can afford it these days, even a hover-car salesman like me."

"Yes, and that's what scares me. The government wants as many people as possible to go through with it, that's why it's relatively cheap... Who knows, eventually this might become compulsory? Maybe in the future we will all be forced to walk around with mechanical brains... It's dehumanizing. This is government mind control at the extreme Johnny. How can you even consider it? Please let it go... for me..."

She smiled and caressed his face with her hand. Her fingers were slender and exquisitely tapered.

"Trust me Johnny, just be happy with who you are. And who knows, perhaps we can fulfil that dream of yours and go visit one of Jupiter's Moons. But we'll have to save up..." She searched his face, looking for reassurance. He managed a smile which seemed to calm her anxiety.

"Right, I've got to go," she said, planting a kiss on his forehead. "I'm meeting Kate in the city centre. Back later..."

Again, she smiled, stood up and left the kitchen swiftly. Johnny remained seated, deep in thought, but the silence of the November day was soon shattered by the sound of the front door opening and closing as Sanny made her way out. He considered what she had said. His mind was being pulled around like a pinball in a machine. He was trying to fight off the urge to go to The Adjustment Group, in order to respect the wishes of his wife. But then an overwhelming desire to see it through took control. He looked at his watch. It read 9.40 am. It was a Saturday. No work today he thought... a perfect moment to go down and visit The Adjustment Group. It would not hurt to at least talk to them about it. He hadn't booked an appointment, but he thought he'd chance it all the same. He could practically feel the hot breath of destiny on his neck. He stood up swiftly, picked up his brown leather jacket and made his way for the door.

As Johnny walked purposefully through the city of New York, hover-cars hummed, circling the sky, slender metallic crafts of countless kinds. Below on the streets, people were everywhere, moving around in a circuitry of motion. It was cold and icy, a typical November day, but it was bright with sunlight. The glorious planet, Earth, as well as all the other circling celestial bodies of the solar system were perpetually bombarded with solar wind blasts, tenuous plasma. There was simply no escape from that variable star, the Sun and today it filled Johnny with a sense of optimism.

He walked on going over and over what Sanny had said to him. For a while, his conscience was getting the better of him, but that soon faded. He had made up his mind, and it was final. He felt compelled to see it through. He began to consider the transplant itself.

"How a biological body can be wired up to a mechanical brain and still function as normal beats me," he muttered to himself, ignoring the questioning glances of the people passing by.

How would it affect one's consciousness, one's perception of reality, one's identity? he thought. He then recalled how some scientists had argued that at death, the mind, consciousness, disconnects from the brain entirely. The symbiotic association ends at death and the mind becomes a free agent. If this was indeed the case, then it would indicate that the real you, your consciousness, your personality, is held in the mind. But again, as far as Johnny was aware, this could not be proven definitively.

Across from him a holographic advertisement suddenly flashed into life. Images of Mars appeared. It was a holiday advertisement: 'FLIGHTS TO MARS.' Many would rush to the red planet. One of its main attractions, Olympus Mons, an enormous shield volcano, over 72,000 ft high, was located in Mars' western hemisphere. He dismissed the scene. Mars held no attraction for him as far as a holiday destination was concerned. Mars Republic was essentially a puritanical culture, and before going, one would need to be inoculated. But the terraformed Moons of Jupiter did appeal. For years he had longed to visit them, Europa in particular, its ocean with its floating settlements, and submarine cities.

Within no time he arrived and behind him surface-vehicles chugged to a halt as they obeyed traffic light signals. Johnny was filled with a sense of awe as he gazed upon the building. It was a tall skyscraper, a great piece of architecture. Its peak soared into the atmosphere but what it contained outweighed all that. Despite his wife's objections he was convinced that this process would only better him. The magazines, the newspapers, the endless TV commercials and the endless hype, had all conspired to give him that confidence that all would be well. This was transhumanism to the extreme, he thought, but he was happy to proceed.

He stepped towards the attractively inviting entrance. Across the thick glass door in gold were the words 'The Adjustment Group, the one and only Transhumanist agency in the world licensed to make drastic brain alterations of cosmological proportions.' He felt awed and humble. Pushing the door open, he entered and saw the figure of a woman, the receptionist. She blended in perfectly with the lush surroundings. He quickly made his way over, his feet beating against the marble floor...

"Good morning, Sir," she chimed, acknowledging him instantly. "Have you an appointment?"

She was tall, slim, and had piercing green eyes, framed by a tumble of brown hair, full red lips. Her soft feminine voice inspired assurance.

"Actually, no... But I'd like to see someone from The Adjustment Group today if possible."

"Sure Sir. Your name...?"

"Johnny Carrasco."

She started to type away briskly on her vid-screen unit which was alive with activity. Upon completion she activated a button. It turned green and pulsed.

"Someone will be with you shortly Mr Carrasco."

Johnny licked his lips. He was getting a little nervous, but it took the form of nervous excitement. He began scanning the surroundings. Everything was neat and polished, exactly what he would expect coming to an elite agency. And for the first time, given his intense focus, he became aware that music was playing in the background, soft and enchanting.

He noticed a family of three, husband, wife and son sitting with a man in a silver-coloured suit. The man was explaining how the mechanical brains were built. Johnny caught bits of the conversation as it drifted to him along with the music in the background. But before he could get the full gist, a thin, grey-haired man came walking over, dressed in a piercing white suit with a yellow tie. He was grinning, a grin that appeared somewhat manufactured.

"Good morning, Mr Carrasco," he said, with all brightness and efficiency. "I'm Dr McLachlan. How can I help you?"

Johnny felt a soothing warmth overwhelm him. He composed himself and replied, "Dr McLachlan, I'm a thirty-four-year-old man who is absolutely fascinated with this whole mechanical brain thing..."

"So much so Mr Carrasco, that you have come here today to the one and only Transhumanist agency in the world wanting the brain transplant," swiftly interjected the doctor.

Johnny smiled.

"Yes indeed, it was a sudden decision. I don't have an appointment."

"Well here at the agency we work on an appointment basis only, but I'll give you a pass. Let's see what I can organize for you today. Please follow me Mr Carrasco."

Time seemed to crawl. Johnny found himself sitting inside Dr McLachlan's office, on the fourth floor, his eyes focusing on objects at random. It was plush and tidy, the sign of a high-profile agency. Documents and files lay neatly arranged on top of a desk, a gold-coloured pen too. After Johnny had been escorted into the office, Dr McLachlan had instructed him to sit and wait while he spoke to the technicians regarding the transplant. He awaited the doctor's return patiently.

In one corner, a large statue of a robot stood out. On the wall was a picture of the eminent computer scientist, Otto Hoffmann. Beneath were the words, *'Space and time are the framework within which the mind is constrained to construct its experience of reality.'* He was the man responsible for building the first mechanical brain which functioned with excellence, mysteriously mimicking the functions of the human brain; a pioneer in the world of AI, Transhumanism. The door swung open. Dr McLachlan stepped in and briskly walked over to his chair. He sat facing Johnny, separated only by the large oak desk, steepling his fingers.

"Right Mr Carrasco, we can proceed with the transplant today. The technicians are preparing accordingly. I must warn you it's a brutal four-hour process."

The slick intercom unit on his desk buzzed, breaking the flow of the conversation. It connected him with the work area of the firm. The sharp petite image of the receptionist's face formed across the screen. "Dr McLachlan, Mr Orson Scott just called. He wants to proceed with the transplant, his wife and kid too. I've booked them all in for tomorrow, 12pm."

"Excellent Ursula, I shall inform the technicians in due course."

The image across the screen skipped and wavered, then vanished...

"As you can see, we are quite busy here at the agency, and more and more people are being drawn to having the life changing transplant. You have made the right decision Mr Carrasco."

Johnny sat there silent and still, arms folded, almost in submission. Dr McLachlan's strong, powerful, voice inspired confidence, total assurance that all would be well...

"Okay before we commence any further, I need you to sign the contract. It contains all the legalities, clauses and so forth, just as one would expect. However, I do need to make certain that you are fully aware of one absolute fact Mr Carrasco."

"Which is?"

"Once the transplant has been completed there is no way of reverting back. Basically, we cannot re-implant biological brains that have been removed. Once you have been wired up to the mechanical brain, a complex and delicate fit, there is simply no way of undoing it. Tampering would result in death. You understand that? So, there's absolutely no way of going back."

Johnny nodded in agreement, but for the first time his eyes suggested that he was tussling with his emotions. After all, no matter how determined he was this was a life altering choice of cosmological proportions. His brain represented what made him him, or at least part of him. Johnny now considered the philosophical implications. He leaned forward, closer to the desk.

"Before I sign the contract, I'd like to ask a few questions."

Dr McLachlan leaned back on his chair suavely, and replied, "Of course that is only natural, Mr Carrasco..."

"Will this robotic, mechanical brain affect my identity, my personality, my perception of space and time in any way?"

Running his fingers through his thick grey hair, Dr McLachlan studied Johnny's face carefully. He consulted his watch, and responded, "Mr Carrasco, firstly, the brain and the mind are separate. You need to make that distinction, it's vital. They are basically two separate yet interconnected entities." He paused and smiled. "Thus, your personality and identity are held in the mind not the brain. The mind is in essence, your soul, your will and emotions, your consciousness. The mind only operates through the brain, which in turn means that the mind can maintain a symbiotic function with a biological brain and also a mechanical one without any issues. It makes no difference to the mind whether it operates through something biological or mechanical. The result is ultimately the same. In short having your biological brain removed and replaced with a mechanical one will not alter your perception of reality, nor will it affect your consciousness or your perception of space and time because it's all in the mind. The real you is your mind, where your entire identity is held and cannot be altered."

"Yes Dr McLachlan, I'm somewhat aware of this philosophical argument, a deep metaphysical subject indeed. But this can't be a proven absolute, can it?"

"Wrong Mr Carrasco! All of my clients that have had the implant are living, breathing proof that personality, identity and consciousness are held in the mind, that mysterious invisible energy that is the real you. A mechanical brain, like a biological brain, is only there to assist the mind, nothing more. Check this out Mr Carrasco... Here at the agency holography is used widely, a unique method of photography, as I'm sure you are well aware, whereby 3D objects are recorded using a laser and then restored as accurately as possible to match the originally recorded subject. When illuminated via laser, holograms are able to form an exact 3D clone of the object and duplicate its features as you are about to see."

Dr McLachlan activated a switch under his desk. He snapped his fingers and pointed towards the corner of the room. Johnny turned his head, his eyes wide and his forehead slightly damp with sweat. A hologram began to form, an oscillating haze that slowly took shape and ballooned into existence. The sharp holographic image of a young, beautiful, dark-haired woman was displayed before them and she did indeed almost look real.

She said, "My name is Sally Smith. I'm thirty years old. I had the transplant and my life changed for the better. My personality and identity have not been affected or altered by the robotic brain transfer in anyway. I feel as real and as me as ever before, enjoying all the benefits that come with the mechanical brain."

The hologram slowly faded. Then another formed, a young man this time.

"My name is Josh Levi. I'm twenty years old. I had the transplant and I've never felt better. It's all me, the mechanical brain has had no effect on my personality or sense of consciousness in anyway. I'm living life to the full as Josh Levi..."

The hologram faded. Johnny turned and focused on Dr McLachlan who sat there with a suave grin.

"Any more questions?" he raised both his hands. "Although, I think this settles the matter. I have hundreds of recorded testimonies Mr Carrasco, hundreds all echoing the same."

Johnny nodded and said, "Yes, I think that settles it."

"Good, now in terms of the mechanical brain... it's humanoid-looking, excellently designed and amazingly functional, made from fine metal, AI working at its best. It will control, with great efficiency, the nervous system, and all the biological processes that take place inside your body. This highly advanced computer is something to behold. Think of it this way... in a sense, biological brains are like computers too, an extremely complex neuroplastic responder. But the advantages of having a mechanical one are endless, as I'm sure you already know..."

"Yes, Dr McLachlan... heightened intellectual capacity, greater memory retention, sharper thought process, and so forth."

"Correct... In a sense you'll be a new person, but at the same time you'll still be you Mr Carrasco."

Johnny rubbed his jaw as if contemplating something else suddenly.

"Dr McLachlan, you called it an extremely complex neuroplastic responder. Just out of interest what do you mean by that exactly?

"Well, this basically means, each time the brain is stimulated by your mind, it responds in various ways, including neurochemical, genetic and electromagnetic changes. This, in turn, grows and changes structures in the brain, building or wiring new physical thoughts..."

"Interesting. But I still don't understand... how can a robotic brain be stimulated by the mind in the same way that a biological brain is?"

"Mr Carrasco, in terms of mechanics, there are going to be operational differences. You are dealing with something mechanical... but ultimately the robotic brain will be stimulated by the mind, attaining the same end result, there's just a different method involved."

"I see..."

"Well without further ado," said the doctor, "it's time for you to sign the contract."

He pushed a file and the gold-coloured pen across the desk.

"Please, the contract is in the file… Take your time."

Johnny opened the file, grabbed the pages and read with absorbed attention, analyzing the data. Minutes passed. Then with a decisive motion, he placed the contract on the desk, picked up the pen and signed. He placed the contract in the file and handed it back to Dr McLachlan.

"Great, now as to the small matter of the payment... A total of 900 credits must be paid prior to the transplant, you understand."

"Of course," replied Johnny. He placed the palm of his left hand on the credit-reader which sat on the desk facing him. It blipped and registered the amount.

"Excellent Mr Carrasco... Finally, before we proceed with the transplant, you'll need to have a brain scan. It won't take long. It's all part of the procedure, protocol. Are you ready?"

It was a brisk three-minute walk through the building to the Transplant Wing, a maze of activity and motion. The scent in the air was that of chemicals. This was where it all happened. Doctors and technicians were standing around holding documents, some with their sleeves rolled up, murmuring and shuffling. He saw a young woman being lead down a corridor, entering a room where her brain was about to be extracted and replaced.

"Right Mr Carrasco, it all happens here. You'll be given a sedative injection prior to the scan. Once the scan is complete, you will then be taken to room C where you will have the transplant. As you already know from the contract, you will be placed into a very deep sleep whilst the transplant takes place."

Johnny acknowledged with a mute nod of his head. Then guided by curiosity he gazed into one of the rooms. The door was wide open and several technicians stood around. He saw an endless line of human brains all placed on a long white table. One by one, the lumps of grey matter were taken by the technicians and placed into black buckets of light blue bubbling liquid.

"I guess the same fate awaits my biological brain, right?" asked Johnny still staring in amazement.

"Yes, that's correct. Essentially, we try and keep the brains alive and conduct various tests on them. It's all part and parcel of the science here. The more we study the mechanisms of the brain, the greater we know. Our understanding can thus evolve and that's vital for this agency. The mind is indeed the most complex thing in the universe, a temporal spatial construct of immense complexity."

Thirty minutes later, Johnny was under minor sedation. He was lying on a machine in a dimly lit room. His head spun. Above him, a large brain-scanner hummed. It was intricate and complex looking, and could move with great flexibility, operating via the aid of a computer. This was all part of the initial phase, he thought. Then the words of the famous philosopher Giordano Campanella returned to him.... 'If all matter consists of quantum fields, then the brain is just a collection of such fields.'

The technician Dr Marconi walked over, peered down at him and asked, "Are you comfortable Mr Carrasco?"

"Yes," he replied, his eyesight somewhat blurred due to the injection, a hard shot of sedative narcotics.

"Any questions before we proceed?"

High and disorientated, but still filled with deep metaphysical questions, despite what he had been told by Dr McLachlan and what the two holographic testimonies had relayed, Johnny was suddenly overwhelmed by vehement emotion and responded, "Dr Marconi, what is consciousness, do you think it's all held in the brain?"

Dr Marconi smiled. "Mr Carrasco, Dr McLachlan told me that he had a long chat with you concerning this subject explaining all that was needed. He even showed you two holographic testimonies. I think the subject matter is settled... Come now..."

Disoriented and riding the high, Johnny's speech was slurred now. He said, "Professor Michael J. Frankland described consciousness as merely the collection of chemical functions in our brains, of neuronal networks of billions of cells communicating with one another. Professor Francis Leibniz, another famous scientist claims that consciousness is not a consequence of interactions between neurons in the brain but arises as from microtubules within cells, which are much smaller and for which quantum effects could be significant."

"Mr Carrasco," said the doctor soothingly, "I could stand here for hours discussing these various theories regarding consciousness, neuronal networks, and microtubules which, as you seem to be aware are molecular assemblies, cylindrical polymers composed of repeating patterns of a single peanut-shaped protein called tubulin that can flex open and closed. I could go on, and on, and on, explaining these various theories. But all you need to know is this... consciousness ultimately exists outside the brain and is held in the mind as Dr McLachlan has explained to you in depth. Now, I need your permission to proceed with the scan. Are you ready?"

"Yes," slurred Johnny.

The technician walked over to his computer, activated a button, and at once, it all commenced, the brain scan was underway. But within seconds of activation, the doctor was left stunned. He gazed at Johnny, then back at the screen, then Johnny, then back at the screen...

The next hour swept by like a lightning strike... Johnny Carrasco was sitting in Dr McLachlan's room once again, tense and worried. He was still battling against the sedative effects of the injection. Confused and perturbed by Dr Marconi's sudden change in behaviour, he wondered what was happening. Once the scan had been completed, Dr Marconi was very quiet, almost subdued. And instead of being taken to room C for the transplant, he was taken back to Dr McLachlan's office. And he didn't know why.

He sat there impatiently, waiting for Dr McLachlan. He wondered why he was there, what they had found, what the problem was. Suddenly the door opened, making him jump and Dr McLachlan walked in and took his seat. He rubbed his head then folded his arms. A strange expression crossed his face. His eyes met Johnny's and held them for a moment. He took a deep breath.

"Mr Carrasco, I've got some shocking news and it won't be easy to take."

He stopped, letting the silence hang. Johnny coughed running fingers through his light brown hair, his eyes staring like two dead coals. He shifted around on his chair a few times in a series of nervous motions.

"Well, what is it Dr McLachlan," he asked anxiously.

"Mr Carrasco you are not who you think you are. And this was all revealed by the eye of a machine."

"I'm sorry what do you mean?"

"You are a robot Mr Carrasco, a complex working functioning android. A top- level machine covered by flesh, obviously built to be more human than human."

Johnny leapt up from his seat, eyes wide... the sedative effects draining away fast from his system and the pitch in his voice rose...

"What are you saying Dr McLachlan?"

"Mr Carrasco, please calm down, I understand this news is hard to take. But unfortunately, this is the reality."

Johnny paced but had nowhere to go so he sat back down, his face now a manifestation of gloom.

"I'm sorry Mr Carrasco but the brain scan has revealed this. Your brain is nothing but a complex piece of mechanical brilliance, serial number AI-4112, somewhat similar to the mechanical brains that we build and implant here. Anyway, we have already refunded you accordingly, 900 credits in full."

"This has got to be a joke?"

"No joke Mr Carrasco I can assure you. We here at The Adjustment Group are also in shock, as well you can imagine. I know that it's hard to take but these are the facts."

"But my body responded to the sedative. That proves I'm human, right?"

"Mr Carrasco, a biomechanical machine would also respond to the drugs just as you did."

The reality of his nature penetrated hard. And he felt it. He held out the palm of his right hand and, moved his fingers back and forth almost mesmerised at the thought that beneath the flesh lay nothing but machinery at work.

He then snapped, "I need proof Dr McLachlan, proof..."

"Proof...? Okay, as you will..."

Dr McLachlan activated a switch from beneath his desk. Moments later the door swung open and technician Dr Marconi walked in.

"Mr Carrasco, please follow me..."

Johnny entered the full body scanning device standing upright and fully clothed, inside the enclosed tube. Dr Marconi activated the machine from a computer terminal. It hummed and began to operate. Bright yellowish light flooded the tube, flashing intermittingly. As the machine started to scan his body, he could see his internal structure displayed before him and it wasn't human, all revealed via a screen that stood in front of him. Johnny's eyes popped and his jaw dropped. For the first time he could see what he truly was, nothing but a machine, an android, built from metal, plastics and flesh, bolts, wires, circuit boards all inter-combined to create a mesh of... of what? He looked on in utter amazement. He battled to compose himself, but it was futile. He was overcome with emotion, mechanical emotion, he thought bitterly, but he felt it all the same as if he were human. He stood staring at his internal structure almost in a trance-like state, languid dream-like thoughts now rippling through his mind. I'm neither man nor robot, an electro domestic, ultimately an inanimate object. I exist in some indescribable limbo.

He focused on his artificial brain, a complex lump of AI, a sophisticated piece of mechanical brilliance, AI at its best, and it looked brain-like but it clearly wasn't organic. It was made up of chips and a maze of intricate wires. He focused hard on it, thinking about the transistors that created a prototype form of consciousness, and the algorithms that regulated the mathematical pathways of his robotic mind... and like an internal earthquake, reality as he had known it crumbled away into a meaningless blur of non-existence from all under the eye of the machine. His robotic mind was a mechanical temple of existential confusion... My so-called reality, emotions and desires are ultimately nothing but a mechanical illusion. Even my desire to visit the Moons of Jupiter isn't real... What now? he thought...

Johnny was escorted back to the office. He fell into his chair as if dead. The brutal reality of his situation struck him like a dagger. He could no longer deny the facts, and his initial unwillingness to accept them faded. The full body scan was complete. It was undeniable. Dr McLachlan searched his face...

"Mr Carrasco, I know that your universe has turned upside down, if you can even call it that, but beyond this we here at The Adjustment Group have nothing more to offer you. We work with humans, not robots. As mentioned, payment has been refunded in full. However, I will leave you with this thought... many philosophers today argue that existence, as a whole, is nothing other than a quantum and virtual anomaly."

Johnny stood up. He composed himself as cold logic replaced emotion and replied, "The philosophical thoughts of Man are vast and complex. We could sit here for hours discussing and dissecting them, indeed we have already to some degree. But the ultimate fact here remains... I am a robot, an android. However, beyond that, you have proven one other thing to me."

"That is?"

"Your agency is responsible for dehumanizing people Dr McLachlan, in essence creating other mini-versions of me. Everything you said prior to the brain scan was nothing but a cleverly manipulated lie. My wife Sanny, whoever she is, whatever she is, and that's another mystery which now needs to be unravelled, was right. The government wants as many people as possible to go through with the transplant, in order to control the masses just like robots, mind control to the very extreme. Eventually it might even become compulsory. Maybe in the future humans will be forced to go through with the process and be dehumanized and become nothing but organic robots, like me."

Dr McLachlan pointed towards the door. Across both cheeks two spots of red glowed. "Mr Carrasco, I have nothing more to say..."

"Indeed, you don't Dr McLachlan. But I walk away from here knowing two things. One I'm a robot, an android, a machine that ironically somewhat understands what it means to be human, and two, whoever walks into this agency will have their soul stripped away and replaced with nothing but a highly advanced computer."

Dr McLachlan now stood up and replied sharply, "I object. You can't compare a robot like you with a human being! You are a soulless machine whose mechanical brain represents the sum of you. But a human, as I have explained, is built differently. A human being has a soul, a mind, and that invisible energy of the mind can operate through both a mechanical brain and biological one and still retain the essence of the person in question. We are not dehumanizing people here Mr Carrasco as you suggest. Please leave..."

Without reply, Johnny turned and walked out.

As Johnny stepped through the door into his house, he noticed his shadow and there he halted staring at it, as if drawn to it for the first time for some unexplainable reason. A strange feeling crept over him and a thought followed... My shadow has no knowledge of me, the shadow is two dimensional. The real me, if I can even call it that, is three dimensional, but both occupy the same space. I might be a machine but there must be other dimensions beyond this, he concluded. Then the familiar smell of coffee and the warm, comfy surroundings of home hit him. Sanny, his wife! Other thoughts came... Is she also a machine, or fully human? If human, how will she react once she finds out that I'm a robot? Or does she already know? If so, who is she? Penetrating fear, electrically induced he realised, crept upon him. Then he heard a sound.

Slowly he walked into the dimly lit living room, gazing around as if he expected there to be changes, but everything was in place; the sofa, the table, the lamp, the lion-ashtray. Everything was as it should be. The wall clock ticked away as always, measuring the silence, and then he noticed Sanny. She stood by the window dressed in a white skirt complemented by her favourite red lipstick. Her bare feet were neatly spaced on the soft white carpet and her blue eyes seemed to lack that warmth that he was so accustomed to seeing. She regarded him impassively, her fingers interlocked.

"Sanny," he said softly, subdued. "We need to talk."

"You went to the agency didn't you Johnny Carrasco? I told you not to."

Reluctantly he replied, "Yes I did..."

Sanny moved away from the window and sat on the cream white sofa. She impaled him with her eyes and said,

"Johnny, your whole existence subsists in a small chip implanted in your head."

"So, you know," he rasped, the colour draining from his drawn face, dark circles under his eyes.

"The company Hiroshi Robotics built a very special android, an android that would lose itself in terms of its identity and thus believe it was human. You are that machine, Johnny. I tried my very best to keep you away from The Adjustment Group. I told you they were a government agency for mind control but you would not listen. Well now you know what you are."

He fell back limply onto the sofa, arms flung aside in dazed horror.

"I work with Hiroshi Robotics. I'm one of the computer scientists there. It's the biggest robotics company in the world with offices scattered all over. Once we built you, you were placed in a home environment and in a sense we created a life for you in order to see how you would adapt under given conditions. We wanted to observe and study how an android, believing it was human, would adapt in a human environment."

He turned and looked at her and said, "So I'm nothing but an experiment?"

"Yes Johnny..."

"And my job as a hover-car salesman, you, me, our life together?"

"Like everything else, we set that up. You are one special robot Johnny Carrasco, programmed, finely tuned with human-like emotions and desires, but ultimately you are nothing but a computerized biomechanical machine, a mass of intricate wires, electrodes, transistors, algorithms, banks of associational neural nets, and flesh, all finely put together. Your augmented memories of the past are nothing but an illusion, all synthetically programmed... an electric fantasy, an artificial construct, false recall including your desire to visit the Moons of Jupiter. You were built to perfection. And I was there to monitor you as your wife and companion. I was appointed to do so. That's the truth..."

"So, what now...?"

"Hiroshi Robotics has made the decision to reverse the process. Now that you have discovered that you are a machine, nothing but a robot, you are going to be modified. That misty metaphysical veil which conceals the real you from the actual you, will once again come into effect. The experiment needs to continue."

Johnny lowered his head. He suddenly felt weak, a sudden depletion of energy.

Sanny stood up and made her way back to the window. The gleaming sunlight soon vanished as thick grey clouds concealed the Sun and the clear blue sky which had accompanied it. Looking at him she said, "Johnny your mechanical system will soon come to a halt. Your synapse and auxiliary memory coils are burning out, deteriorating. Your motor system is shutting down. The transistors that create a prototype form of consciousness will soon fail, and the algorithms that regulate the mathematical pathways of your robotic mind will soon cease. The process is already underway, triggered from afar via a computer terminal which in essence keeps you alive... if you can call it that."

"No, I'm real," he suddenly yelled as if an internal existential battle had suddenly exploded within the very depths of his mechanical being, something similar to human cognitive dissonance. "It's all just a question of psychology, cognitive psychology, regardless of whether I'm a machine or human, or a mix of both. If I believe I'm real, real I am. As Rene Descartes said, I think, therefore I am. Everything that exists moulds an image of that space in which it lives. Mind controls the formation of matter, mechanical or biological. Destroy those minds and all matter fades away like sand lost in the ocean of time.

Whatever exists in the universe shall, and will always exist, regardless of my fate..."

Induced by failing mechanical glands, small complex bundles of wires, his electrical thought impulses became distorted, just like an adrenaline rush would distort them in a human mind. Then, within a fraction of a second, everything around him appeared to liquefy and fade into a distorted, shapeless blur, suffused with a pale, milky luminescence. The ticking wall clock, the table, the lamp and the lion-ashtray were the first to go, then a section of the room. If I think hard enough perhaps everything will come back, he thought, but that was just wishful thinking. Sanny was now nothing but a ghostly glimmering, meaningless blur of semi-nonexistence, twisting within the depths of his fading mechanical mind. He attempted to stretch time but that was metaphysically impossible. He heard a loud buzzing sound that seemed to come from everywhere. Stars and nebulae poured past him in an illusion of infinite speed. The colossal powers that were lodged in his robotic brain were ceasing and the universe he had known trembled and shattered before him. Then as if space, time and matter had collapsed around him, he was seemingly transported into a dark vacuum.

Sanny shrugged and switched on the small Tele-set... An advert flashed into life. Audio followed. 'Call The

Adjustment Group, the one and only Transhumanist agency in the world licensed to make drastic brain alterations of cosmological proportions.'

Johnny's eyes widened...

Galactic Voyages

The process fascinated him. Temporal Transference they called it. Thirty-year-old Clint Schwarzenbeck stood inside a translucent capsule where icy air circled around him, electrodes neatly covering the frontal region of his head. His heartbeat began to increase due to the high levels of narcotics that pumped through his system and a swollen vein throbbed at his temple.

This transportation device was revolutionary. It had stretched the laws of science. Only the privileged, the mega-rich, were able to enjoy such a unique metaphysical experience. The art of sending one's consciousness back and forth across space had been mastered. The philosophical implications that came with the journey could only be defined in metaphysical terms. Galactic Voyages was the company that had created the technology and Dr Van Schip was one of the main scientists behind the earth-shattering invention... non-physical space travel.

Dr Van Schip, an exotic thinker, believed since consciousness was not physical, it bypassed all the problems that came with physical space travel. And there were many. Potential asteroid collisions were always a concern. Not to mention boredom and galloping claustrophobia due to the time it would take to reach far off destinations. Long haul journeys across space would drag to the extreme. As a result, space psychosis was not unheard of. Then there was the problem of cosmic rays, those extremely high-energy subatomic particles, protons and atomic nuclei, that move through space at nearly the speed of light. Radiation poisoning was a major concern for space travellers. The damages it caused to the body were potentially lethal, inducing cancer, damage to the central nervous system, and so forth. Engineers and scientists alike had tried to overcome the problem and to some degree they had made significant steps. The outer hulls of most spaceships were built to stop almost anything in the electromagnetic spectrum, but sadly the hardest radiation would still seep through. As for wormholes in space, these ideas were too fantastic to be taken seriously.

And so, Clint Schwarzenbeck's consciousness was now destined for Callisto, one of Jupiter's terraformed Moons. The ocean world had always fascinated him with its submarine cities and floating settlements, and it was one those floating settlements where he would arrive at. He couldn't wait. The process was this: his consciousness, the fundamental nature of his being, would leave his body, traverse space, and enter into a humanoid. This humanoid was a machine, a robot covered by skin that looked human. This was the universal method deployed by Galactic Voyages for all its clients; human consciousness entered into a humanoid body that looked more human than human, a skin covered avatar, in order to enjoy a unique experience, an enthralling fusion. Thousands of these humanoids had been built by the company across the galaxy at different locations such as Mars, Europa, Ganymede, and of course Callisto and beyond... It was big business. Clint Schwarzenbeck would soon occupy one of these humanoids, an empty, skin- covered, lifeless robot that awaited his life force.

Dr Dimitrios Nikolopoulos activated a switch as lights flashed and flickered around the giant chamber, a maze of machinery. Computers worked away registering and supplying vital bits of data that pertained to Clint's bodily functions. Meters swung into activity. Inside the transparent capsule where Clint stood dressed in a light grey one-piece suit which the company had provided, there was a hum and a surge of energy, followed by a beam of blue light which fell upon him. His head jolted in spasm, his heart raced, and he was away, the universe moving in obedience; mind had freed itself from matter. The body that remained in the capsule was now nothing but an empty vessel which would be kept alive inside the capsule until consciousness returned. He would be gone for around seventeen Earth days, roughly, a day on Callisto and this added to the excitement.

Seconds later, his consciousness collected around the machine body. The frenzied bundle of random impulses soon melted away. Logical processes were restored, and all at once the world became three dimensional again. During his trip he experienced all tenses in a white blur of energy that seemed to house the past, present and future. He opened his eyes with joyful triumph, his consciousness was now housed inside a humanoid, an avatar. He stood inside yet another capsule, upright, just like he had on his departure from Earth. Only this time the capsule was not transparent and he could not see beyond it. He moved his hands and feet as if it were his own body, his conscious mind sending out something similar to a motor impulse. He smiled as he adjusted to it accordingly. He felt comfortable.

'I am here on Callisto,' he marvelled, 'living inside a well-built, skin-covered humanoid that looks more human than human.' There would be no conflict between his mind and the machine; his consciousness and the humanoid would work together in symbiosis.

Suddenly the capsule started to part. As it opened, he caught sight of a robot, and behind it, a large flashing sign...Galactic Voyages. He stepped out accompanied by a miasma of strange mist...

"Welcome to Callisto Mr Schwarzenbeck," said the tall metallic robot. "Here at Galactic Voyages, we want the best for all our clients. So please enjoy your stay here. We look forward to seeing you later for your rest period, if you choose."

Clint grinned and walked across the light flooded chamber towards the exit feeling an unfamiliar lightness in the lower gravity. He allowed the various sensations of the room to pour over him, giving him the feeling of being fully human, even though he wasn't. After all the definition of human was consciousness housed inside a biological body, a biological system, a complex symbiotic network of flesh and blood. Before he exited the chamber, he caught sight of a large mirror. He turned gazing at himself, but paradoxically it wasn't really him, at least externally speaking. The humanoid, the avatar which housed his consciousness was so human-like it was quite extraordinary. He was tall, athletic, with dark hair and bright blue eyes, dressed in a slick white outfit. Truth was, the real him, his human body, which was back on Earth, looked completely different. He made brief comparisons... His real flesh and blood body was slightly out of shape and he wasn't particularly tall. His eyes were dark brown, and his hair was blond.

Clint exited and within three minutes could see the indoor city centre ahead. There were people everywhere, robots too. And there were shops and bars scattered all around, all within this huge floating city. His dream had been fulfilled. Callisto had always been his golden destination. Other places had never appealed to him for various reasons. Mars Republic was essentially a puritanical culture where they didn't even practice sex and the official language was

German. Not to mention that all the restaurants on Mars demanded abnormally huge tips from all its tourists, a necessary lubricant in order to get first class service. As for Ganymede, well it didn't actually have laws as such, just company regulations, none of which seemed concerned with personal conduct. Aside from that, it was renowned for being boring, expensive, and there was little in the form of entertainment. Venus was known for its corrupt government; a heartless, malevolent living organism. The Elite Venus Corporation ran and owned everything. If you had the right connections, you could literally get away with murder. Aside from that it was also known for its luxury air-pumped hotels, the rooms containing so many complex gadgets that one would need a degree in engineering before taking a shower and if you wanted to visit the outside world, the main city Venusville for instance, you would have to walk around with gloves and an oxygen mask due to the thick, toxic atmosphere filled with carbon dioxide.

He looked out through the thick glass window that separated settlement from sea. Jupiter was not visible due to their positioning. Callisto was tidally locked with the Gas Giant, and they were located on the far-side of the moon. The night sky was something to behold. Then he caught sight of a ship, a tiny, complex toy floating inert in the void, over a volume of space. He scanned the sea, miles and miles of water twisting and turning turbulently. Then, in the far distance, he noticed two other settlements, huge indoor floating worlds that housed thousands and thousands of colonists from Earth. In the night darkness, the brightly lit settlements shined like lanterns. Suddenly an amplified female voice blared, '*A large ice asteroid impacted Mars causing dust storms and minor quakes to trouble Olympus base.*' It was a news bulletin. The sound came from all directions via large speakers with finesse and clarity, echoing throughout the indoor world.

Right, time to explore this floating city he thought. He walked on, gazing around curiously. After a couple of minutes, he halted in his tracks. Something caught his attention. It was a bright flashing sign which read...'*Visit Aristotle's Chamber for a Cosmic Journey of a life-time...*' He grinned, rubbed his forehead and wondered what this was all about. The great Greek philosopher's name was even known on Callisto. He was deeply intrigued. He walked down a brightly lit corridor with low gravity steps, eventually reaching a gleaming brass door. Above the door, written in silver, were the words, '*Retrocausal quantum theory implies that time can flow backwards...*' Clint was deeply curious. He wanted to discover more. Via sensors the door opened automatically in vertical motion. He stepped into an enormous room, the floor sparkling with glacial crystal. It resembled a Greek temple, and his attention was immediately drawn to a big white spherical machine. A thin white mist swam across it. The words, 'Aristotle's Chamber,' were etched in gold onto the machine's frame.

On the wall behind it, was a picture of planet Earth framed in outer space. Beneath in bold it read, *'Gravity on a Neutron star is 2 billion times stronger than on Earth. It's strong enough to bend radiation from stars in a process known as gravitational lensing.'* Then he noticed another picture. It was a picture of the Milky Way. Beneath it read, *'Only in an infinitesimally small fraction of the total Creation are the parameters such that matter can exist, stars can form, and life as we know it arises.'*

He jumped slightly as a bronzed man dressed in a blue outfit, his hair brown, evenly parted seemed to have appeared from out of nowhere.

"Welcome to Aristotle's Chamber. I'm Von Hessen," he said...

Clint, somewhat startled, could only stare for a moment. Then he waved his arms vaguely and asked, "What is this exactly?"

"It's a sophisticated supercomputer, a robot that can answer the most complex scientific and philosophical questions almost before you ask them. In short, Aristotle's Chamber can carry out any routine mathematical operation. Simply ask it a question and it will give you a detailed answer; the sharpest computer you'll ever meet... with great flexible logic."

"Really...?"

"Yes, basically it's a living entity in its own right, and you can trust it too. Unlike the other computers that were installed to function in the same capacity, this one's completely honest. And with a mere 100 Callisto Credits you can experience something quite unique, a Cosmic Journey of a life-time."

In the moments of silence that followed, Aristotle's Chamber started to hum and its door opened vertically, almost as if it knew that it was about to go to work. He could hear the sound of switching circuits.

"You're from Earth, aren't you?" said Von Hessen suddenly.

"Yes, correct..."

"What's your name?"

"Clint Schwarzenbeck..."

"Galactic voyages brought you here?"

"Yes they did..."

"All the humanoids that they use to house consciousness are so easy to spot. Don't get me wrong, you almost look human, almost... But the inorganic eyes always give it away."

Clint smiled, and the humanoid's lips moved symbiotically, responding to his being and it felt so natural.

"Temporal Transference has revolutionized the world," said Von Hessen eagerly. "It's the greatest scientific breakthrough the world has ever seen. The only thing that comes close to it is time travel. Mankind has always dreamt of travelling through the fourth dimension, bending the space-time continuum, forming a wormhole, but temporal transference beats it by a distance."

"So where do I pay?" said Clint gazing excitedly at the machine.

Von Hessen pointed. "The credit-register there on the side, just before you enter."

Clint stepped towards the chamber and placed the palm of his left hand, the humanoid's hand, on the credit-register. A special payment chip had been implanted into the humanoid which was connected to Clint's account. The credit-register blipped and he entered the brightly lit chamber. A large screen stood before him, close by, a comfortable looking black chair. He dropped into it and looked towards the screen expectantly. The door closed automatically and the light faded to black. Then the screen came alive; a thousand points of the light illuminated the chamber, causing him to shield his eyes for a moment. A face formed across the screen, a manifestation of mechanical forces. Warmed with energy, artificial neurons began to fire. It looked humanoid and its fiery eyes held something beyond explanation. Its slumbering powers had been awakened.... Clint's consciousness drifted into full focus.

"Greetings, Mr Schwarzenbeck. I'm Aristotle. Please ask your first question," it said with a refined male voice, a voice that seemed to come from everywhere.

Clint rubbed his head, perplexed. He wondered how the computer knew his name. Was it psychic? he suddenly thought.

"Mr Schwarzenbeck," said Aristotle, "With regard to your name, the information was relayed to me via the payment chip, via the credit-register."

Clint smiled. This computer was not only meant to be a fountain of knowledge, but it was also intuitive, perceptive, multi-evaluating, it could read people as it had done him. It was alive alright, self-aware. Psychologists assert this happens automatically whenever a brain, biological or mechanical, acquires a certain very high number of associational paths. Clint once again felt in control of the situation. The computer was not psychic after all, giving him a perfectly logical, rational explanation as to how it knew his name. But it could certainly read minds, he thought in jest.

Aristotle then said, "Via your payment chip, I also now know that you are from Earth."

"That's correct."

"And that Galactic voyages brought you here... Temporal Transference is what they call it... the art of sending one's consciousness back and forth across space. Your consciousness Mr Schwarzenbeck has been housed inside an avatar, the very one sitting here before me."

"Yes... that's right."

"Well, this makes for quite an interesting session don't you think?"

Clint smiled... It was kind of ironic. He was a human being housed inside a robot, a skin-covered machine that was talking to another highly advanced machine.

"Okay Mr Schwarzenbeck, please ask your first question..."

Clint leaned back in his chair, composed himself, and being a lover of science, space and philosophy randomly selected his first question...

"Aristotle, tell me about cosmic rays."

"Certainly... Cosmic rays are atom fragments that rain down on the Earth from outside the solar system, high-energy protons and atomic nuclei that move through space at nearly the speed of light. They originate from the Sun, from outside of the solar system in our own galaxy, and from distant galaxies. They also attract tremendous interest practically, due to the damage they cause on microelectronics and life outside the protection of an atmosphere and magnetic field."

He was impressed. He leaned forward... "Tell me about Solar Winds."

"Solar wind is a stream of charged particles released from the upper atmosphere of the Sun which is called the corona. This plasma consists of mostly electrons, protons and alpha particles with kinetic energy. The sun's corona reaches startling temperatures of up to two million degrees Fahrenheit. At this level, the sun's gravity can't hold on to the rapidly moving particles, and they stream away from the star. The sun's activity shifts over the course of its 11-year cycle, with sun spot numbers, radiation levels, and ejected material changing over time. These alterations affect the properties of the solar wind, including its velocity, magnetic field, temperature and density. The wind also differs based on where from the sun it comes and how quickly that portion is rotating."

Clint was fascinated and asked another random question, "What do Spiral Galaxies consist of?"

"Mr Schwarzenbeck, spiral galaxies have three visible parts: a thin disk composed of stars, gas and dust, a central bulge of older stars and a spherical halo of the oldest stars and massive star clusters. The signature of these galaxies is an elegant spiral pattern in the disk."

"Yes, but how is a spiral galaxy formed Aristotle?"

"I believe that a galaxy's spiral structure originates as a density wave emanating from the galactic centre. The idea is that the entire disk of a galaxy is filled with material. The spiral arms of a galaxy mark where in the galaxy the density wave recently passed, causing new stars to form and burn brightly.

"Okay, so that's pretty general. Tell me a little bit about the Andromeda Galaxy Aristotle."

"The Andromeda Galaxy, also known as Messier 31, is a barred spiral galaxy approximately 2.5 million light-years from your planet Earth and the nearest large galaxy to the Milky Way, with a diameter of around 220,000 ly. The number of stars contained in the Andromeda Galaxy is estimated at one trillion. The virial mass of the Andromeda Galaxy is of the same order of magnitude as that of the Milky Way at 1 trillion solar masses. Furthermore, the Andromeda Galaxy was formed approximately 10 billion years ago from the collision and subsequent merger of smaller protogalaxies. The violent collision formed most of the galaxy's metal-rich, galactic halo and extended disk. During this epoch, its rate of star formation would have been very high, to the point of becoming a luminous infrared galaxy for roughly 100 million years. The Andromeda Galaxy is also known to harbour a dense and compact star cluster at its very centre. Finally, the Milky Way and Andromeda galaxies are expected to collide in around 4-5 billion years, merging to form a giant elliptical galaxy or a large lenticular galaxy."

Clint laughed and clapped his hands together in delight. This was proving to be an enlightening experience. He decided to change tack a little.

"Okay Aristotle... Tell me something interesting about say... Pluto."

The computer replied, "Icy Pluto, the dwarf planet is a very mysterious complex world containing valleys, mountains, craters, and plains. It isn't known exactly whether Pluto has a magnetic field, but its small size and slow rotation suggest little or none. In terms of its size, Pluto is only about 1,400 miles wide. It is approximately 3.6 billion miles away from the Sun, and it has a thin atmosphere which is composed mostly of nitrogen, methane, and also carbon monoxide. On average, Pluto's temperature is -387 Fahrenheit, which is -232 Celsius. At this temperature it is far too cold to sustain life. Furthermore, Pluto is orbited by five known moons. The largest is Charon which is about half the size of Pluto itself, making it the largest satellite relative to the planet it orbits in our solar system. Due to this, Pluto and Charon are often referred to as a 'double planet.' Furthermore, Charon orbits Pluto at a distance of just 12,200 miles, and its orbit around Pluto takes 153 hours, the same time it takes Pluto to complete one rotation. This in turn means, Charon neither rises nor sets but hovers over the same spot on Pluto's surface at all times. And the same side of Charon always faces Pluto, that is, it is tidally-locked. The other four moons, Nix, Styx, Kerberos, and Hydra are much smaller, less than 100 miles wide. They are also irregularly shaped, not spherical like Charon. And unlike Charon these four moons are not tidally locked to Pluto.

In terms of the potential for life... the surface of Pluto is very cold, extremely so, thus it is unlikely that life could exist there. At such cold temperatures, water, which is vital for life as we know it, is essentially rock-like. With a radius of 715 miles, Pluto is approximately 1/6 the width of your planet, Earth. From an average distance of 3.7 billion miles, icy Pluto is 39 astronomical units away from the Sun. One astronomical unit is the distance from the Sun to Earth. From this distance, it takes sunlight 5.5 hours to travel from the Sun to Pluto. For example, if you were to stand on the surface of Pluto at noon, the Sun would be 1/900 the brightness it is on your planet, Earth. There is a moment each day near sunset on your planet Earth when the light is the same brightness as midday on Pluto. Pluto's orbit around the Sun is unusual compared to the planets. It is both elliptical and tilted. Pluto's 248 year long, oval-shaped orbit can take it as far as 49.3 astronomical units from the Sun, and as close as 30 AU. One day on Pluto takes approximately 153 hours. Its axis of rotation is tilted at 57 degrees with respect to the plane of its orbit around the Sun, thus it spins almost on its side. Pluto also exhibits a retrograde rotation, spinning from east to west just like the rock planet Venus and the gas planet, Uranus.

Now with regard to its formation... Pluto, the dwarf planet is a member of a group of objects that orbit in a disc-like zone beyond the orbit of Neptune called the Kuiper Belt. This distant realm is populated with thousands of miniature icy worlds, which formed approximately 4.5 billion years ago. These icy, rocky bodies are called Kuiper Belt objects. Pluto has a thin, tenuous atmosphere that expands when it comes closer to the Sun and collapses as it moves farther away. When Pluto is close to the Sun, its surface ices sublimate changing from solid to gas, and rise to temporarily form a thin atmosphere.

Finally, Pluto's surface is very fascinating indeed. Its tallest mountains are 6,500 to 9,800 feet in height. The mountains are in essence huge blocks of water ice, sometimes with a coating of frozen gases such as methane, etc. Other interesting features on the dwarf planet are the long troughs and valleys. Interestingly craters as large as 161 miles in diameter dot some of the complex landscape on the dwarf planet Pluto, with some showing signs of erosion and filling. This in turn suggests that tectonic forces are slowly resurfacing Pluto."

Clint stared in wonder at the machine before him. "Tell me about Alpha Centauri..."

"Indeed... Alpha Centauri is a gravitationally bound system of the closest stars and exoplanets to our Solar System at 4.37 light-years from the Sun. Alpha Centauri is a triple star system, with its two main stars, Alpha Centauri A and Alpha Centauri B, together comprising a binary component. The A and B components of Alpha Centauri have an orbital period of 79.91 years. Their orbit is moderately eccentric, their closest approach or periastron is 11.2 AU, or about the distance between the Sun and Saturn... and their furthest separation or apastron is 35.6 AU, about the distance between the Sun and Pluto."

"That will do Aristotle." Clint discovered he had many more questions than he had originally thought. The joy of just firing off any question that popped into his head and having it answered in detail was intoxicating.

"So, next question... How would you describe quantum mechanics?"

"Quantum mechanics is a fundamental theory in physics that provides a description of the physical properties of nature at the scale of atoms and subatomic particles. Basically, it is the foundation of all quantum physics including quantum chemistry, quantum field theory, quantum technology, and so forth."

Clint's mind shot off in yet another direction and he asked, "What about the moon, Phobos..."

"An exotic question Mr Schwarzenbeck... This moon is the innermost and larger of the two natural satellites of Mars, the other being Deimos. Phobos is a small, irregularly shaped object with a mean radius of 11 km. It orbits 6,000 km from the Martian surface, closer to its primary body than any other known planetary moon. It is so close that it orbits Mars much faster than Mars rotates, completing its orbit in just seven hours and thirty-nine minutes. As a result, from the surface of Mars it appears to rise in the west, move across the sky in four hours and fifteen minutes, and set in the east, twice each Martian day."

"Okay... what about Deimos?"

"Well, that moon is the smaller and outermost of the two natural satellites of Mars. Deimos has a mean radius of 6.2 km and takes 30.3 hours to orbit Mars."

"Sooo... If a person on Earth weighs 100kg, how much would that person weigh on the surface of Mars?"

"Because of the lower gravity, that person who weighs 100kg on Earth would only weigh 38kg on the surface of Mars."

"Tell me about Earth's moon..."

"Earth's Moon.... mysterious indeed, even these days. The Moon is a differentiated body that was initially in hydrostatic equilibrium but has since departed from this condition. It has a geochemically distinct crust, mantle, and core. The Moon has a solid iron-rich inner core with a radius possibly as small as 240 kilometres and a fluid outer core primarily made of liquid iron with a radius of approximately 300 kilometres. Isotope dating of lunar samples suggests the Moon formed around 50 million years after the origin of the solar system. Thus, the Moon formed about 4.51 billion years ago. Furthermore, Earth's Moon lacks any significant atmosphere, hydrosphere, or magnetic field. Its surface gravity is about one-sixth of Earth's. Orbiting Earth at an average distance of 384,400 km, its gravitational influence slightly lengthens Earth's day and is the main driver of Earth's tides. The Moon's orbit around Earth has a sidereal period of 27.3 days. During each synodic period of 29.5 days, the amount of visible surface illuminated by the Sun varies from none up to 100%, resulting in lunar phases that form the basis for the months of a lunar calendar. Furthermore, the Moon is tidally locked to Earth, which means that the length of a full rotation of the Moon on its own axis causes its same side to always face Earth. However, that said, 59% of the total lunar surface can be seen from Earth through shifts in perspective due to libration. The Earth-Moon system formed after a giant impact of a Mars-sized body with the proto-Earth. The impact blasted material into orbit about the Earth and then the material accreted and formed the Moon. With regard to its surface geology, its most extensive topographic feature is the giant far-side South Pole-Aitken basin, some 2,240 km in diameter, the largest crater on the Moon and the second-largest confirmed impact crater in the Solar System. At 13 km deep, its floor is the lowest point on the surface of the Moon. The highest elevations of the Moon's surface are located directly to the northeast, which might have been thickened by the oblique formation impact of the South Pole-Aitken basin. Finally, Lunar swirls are mysterious features found across the Moon's surface, which are characterized by having a high albedo, appearing optically immature and having a sinuous shape. Their curvilinear shape is often accentuated by low albedo regions that wind between the bright swirls. They appear to overlay the lunar surface, superposed on top of craters and ejecta deposits..."

Clint was absorbing the data like a sponge.

"Neutron Stars... tell me about those."

"Well Mr Schwarzenbeck neutron stars are formed when a massive star runs out of fuel and collapses. The core of the star collapses, the central region, crushing together every proton and electron into a neutron. Thus, in short, a neutron star is the collapsed core of a massive supergiant star, which incidentally had a total mass of between 10 and 25 solar masses, possibly even more if the star was especially metal-rich. Except for black holes, and some hypothetical objects like quark stars, neutron stars are the smallest and densest class of stellar objects. They have a radius on the order of 10 kilometres and a mass of approximately 1.4 solar masses. They result from the supernova explosion of a massive star, combined with gravitational collapse that compresses the core past white dwarf star density to that of atomic nuclei. As the star's core collapses its rotation rate increases as a result of conservation of angular momentum, and newly formed neutron stars hence rotate at up to several hundred times per second. In fact, some neutron stars emit beams of electromagnetic radiation that make them detectable as pulsars. Furthermore, neutron stars are composed almost entirely of neutrons, basically subatomic particles with no net electrical charge and with slightly larger mass than protons; the electrons and protons present in normal matter combine to produce neutrons at the conditions in a neutron star..."

"Tell me about Quantum tunnelling..." said Clint focusing hard on the humanoid face across the screen.

"Another excellent question," replied Aristotle with human-like vocal reflexes... "Well basically, Quantum tunnelling is a phenomenon where an atom or a subatomic particle can appear on the opposite side of a barrier that should be impossible for the particle to penetrate. Another way to define it is that Quantum Tunnelling is the quantum mechanical phenomenon where a wavefunction can propagate through a potential barrier. Furthermore, the transmission through the barrier can be finite and depends exponentially on the barrier height and barrier width. The wavefunction may disappear on one side and reappear on the other side. The wavefunction and its first derivative are continuous..."

Clint's grasshopper mind lurched to another question.

"Right... tell me about Quantum Magnetic Levitation. How does it work?"

"Mr Schwarzenbeck, the levitation works thanks to superconductivity, which could be understood through basic principles of conductivity. Certain elements and materials, aptly called conductors, serve as an electrical conduit, which means electrons can pass through them with relative ease. Furthermore, these electrons still knock into the atoms that make up the conductor and thus lose a bit of energy with each collision. But, when cooled to a sufficiently cold temperature, the electrons can flow freely with ease through the conductor without any collisions... That's because electrons pair up at extremely low temperatures... whereas heat would break the tentative bond between them... Although their bonds are weak, there is strength in numbers... Pairing up makes it so the collisions that would normally leech energy from the electron flow have no effect because the collisions are weaker than the electrons' bond... Thus, in short, quantum magnetic levitation comes down to something called the Meissner effect, which only occurs when a material is cold enough to behave like a superconductor. At normal temperatures, magnetic fields can pass through the material normally. Once it is cold enough to exhibit superconductivity, however, those magnetic fields get expelled. Any magnetic fields that were passing through must instead move around it. When a magnet is placed above a superconductor at critical temperature, the superconductor pushes away its field by acting like a magnet with the same pole causing the magnet to repel, that is, float..."

"Okay, tell me something fascinating about Mercury."

"Planet Mercury, named after the Roman god Mercurius, is the smallest planet in the solar system, only slightly larger than Earth's Moon, and nearest to the Sun. Despite its proximity to the Sun, Mercury is not the hottest planet in our solar system... that title belongs to nearby Venus, due to its dense atmosphere. The surface temperature of Mercury ranges from 100 to 700 K, -173 to 427 Celsius. From the surface of Mercury, the Sun would appear more than three times as large as it does when viewed from Earth, and the sunlight would be as much as seven times brighter. Now due to Mercury's elliptical orbit, and slow-moving rotation, the Sun appears to rise briefly, set, and rise again from some parts of the planet's surface. The same thing happens in reverse at sunset. Its orbit around the Sun takes 87.97 Earth days, the shortest of all the Sun's planets. Mercury appears to have a solid silicate crust and mantle overlying a solid, iron sulfide outer core layer, a deeper liquid core layer, and a solid inner core. The planet's density is the second highest in the Solar System... in fact Mercury's core has a higher iron content than that of any other major planet in the Solar System. Its surface is similar in appearance to that of the Earth's Moon, showing extensive mare-like plains and heavy cratering, indicating that it has been geologically inactive for billions of years. Furthermore, Mercury was heavily bombarded by comets and asteroids during and shortly following its formation 4.6 billion years ago. It received impacts over its entire surface during this period of intense crater formation, facilitated by the lack of any atmosphere to slow impactors down. During this time the planet was volcanically active... basins were filled by magma. Now craters on Mercury range in diameter from small bowl-shaped cavities to multi-ringed impact basins hundreds of kilometres across. In terms of gravity, magnetic field and magnetosphere, Mercury is too small and hot for its gravity to retain any significant atmosphere over long periods of time. It does have a tenuous surface-bound exosphere which contains hydrogen, helium, oxygen, potassium, calcium, sodium, etc, at a surface pressure of less than approximately 0.5 nPa... Hydrogen and helium atoms probably come from the solar wind, diffusing into Mercury's magnetosphere before later escaping back into space. Radioactive decay of elements within Mercury's crust is another source of helium, as well as sodium and potassium. Now despite its small size and slow, 59-day long rotation, Mercury has a significant magnetic field. The magnetic-field strength at Mercury's equator is about 300 nT. Like that of planet Earth, Mercury's magnetic field is dipolar. Furthermore, the planet's magnetic field is strong enough to deflect the solar wind around the planet, creating a magnetosphere. The planet's magnetosphere is strong enough to trap solar wind plasma... This contributes to the space weathering of the planet's surface. Finally, Planet Mercury has the most eccentric orbit of all the planets in the Solar System. Its eccentricity is 0.21 with its distance from the Sun, the giant nuclear reactor, ranging from 46,000,000 to 70,000,000 km..."

The asteroid belt had always fascinated Clint and now he leaned forward eagerly and said, "Tell me a little bit about the asteroid belt Aristotle..."

"The asteroid belt is a torus-shaped region in the Solar System. It is located between the orbits of the planets Jupiter and Mars. Furthermore, the asteroid belt is the smallest and innermost known circumstellar disc in the Solar System. Around half its mass is contained in the four largest asteroids... and they are Ceres, Pallas, Vesta and Hygiea. The total mass of the asteroid belt is approximately 4% that of the Moon, Earth's Moon that is. Ceres, the only object in the asteroid belt large enough to be a dwarf planet, is about 951 km in diameter. Vesta, Pallas and Hygiea have mean diameters of less than 600 km. With regard to the remaining bodies, they range down to the size of a dust particle. The asteroid material is so thinly distributed that numerous spacecraft have traversed it without any incident. Contrary to popular thought, the asteroid belt is mostly empty. The asteroids are spread over such a large volume that it would be improbable to reach an asteroid without aiming carefully. However, collisions between large asteroids do occur. In terms of composition... the belt consists primarily of three categories of asteroids... C-type, S-type, and M-type... C-type, carbonaceous asteroids, are carbon-rich and they dominate the asteroid belt's outer regions. Together they comprise over 75% of the visible asteroids and they are redder in hue than the other asteroids and have a very low albedo. S-type, silicate-rich asteroids are more common toward the inner region of the belt, within 2.5 AU of the Sun. The spectra of their surfaces reveal the presence of silicates and some metal, but no significant carbonaceous compounds. Finally, M-type, metal-rich asteroids form around 10% of the total population... their spectra resemble that of iron-nickel. Some formed from the metallic cores of differentiated progenitor bodies that were disrupted through collision..."

"Great," said Clint satisfied. "So, now tell me a little bit about the speed of light... That fascinates me..."

"The speed of light travelling through a vacuum is exactly 299,792,458 meters per second... which approximately equates to 186,000 miles per second or 300,000 kilometres per second, a universal constant known in equations as 'c' or light speed. Thus, the speed of light in vacuum, denoted 'c' is a universal physical constant. Now according to special relativity, c is the upper limit for the speed at which conventional matter, energy or any signal carrying information can travel through space. Furthermore, all forms of electromagnetic radiation travel at the speed of light.... not just the visible spectrum. Massless particles and field perturbations such as gravitational waves also travel at this speed in vacuum. Such particles and waves travel at c regardless of the motion of the source or the inertial reference frame of the observer. Additionally, particles with nonzero rest mass can approach c, but can never actually reach it... Furthermore, in quantum physics, the electromagnetic field is described by the theory of quantum electrodynamics. In this theory, light is described by the fundamental excitations or quanta of the electromagnetic field, called photons. In quantum electrodynamics, photons are massless particles and thus, according to special relativity, they travel at the speed of light in vacuum. Finally, in a medium, light usually does not propagate at a speed equal to c. The phase velocity is important in determining how a light wave travels through a material. It is often represented in terms of a refractive index. The refractive index of a material is defined as the ratio of c to the phase velocity v/p in the material: larger indices of refraction indicate lower speeds. Now, the refractive index of a material may depend on the light's frequency, polarization, direction of propagation, or intensity."

Clint sat back. It had been great fun so far and he had learned a lot but essentially, he had been asking questions that he could have found the answer to in any encyclopaedic platform. This machine was meant to be so much more than that. It was time to up the ante, and test its reasoning. Seconds of silence passed, the machine humming patiently in the background while he tried to formulate a question that might stretch its abilities.

"Okay Aristotle, I now want to ask you a few philosophical questions... Firstly, does time really exist? Is time nothing but an illusion, something created to make sense of the universe?"

"Before I give you an answer," said Aristotle, "let me say this... Many philosophers and physicists on Earth suspect that time is not fundamental... rather, time emerges out of something more fundamental... something non-temporal... One top philosopher back on Earth states, *'What reality is depends on what time is. Is time irreducible, fundamental, an ultimate descriptor of bedrock reality? Or is our subjective sense of flowing time, generated by our brains that evolved for other purposes, an illusion?'* Another believes, *'Time is only a reflection of change. From change, our brains construct a sense of time as if it were flowing. All the evidence we have for time is encoded in static configurations, which we see or experience subjectively, all of them fitting together to make time seem linear...'* Finally, the great scientist, physicist, Arthur C. Wells stated, *'It is a mistaken argument to use relativity to assert that time is an illusion, because no observer has knowledge of a distant event, or the simultaneity of different events, until they are unambiguously in that observer's past. And, therefore, that argument focuses on the way observers organize their description of the past and cannot establish the reality of the awaiting future.*

Thus, Mr Schwarzenbeck we can portray reality as either a three-dimensional place where things happen over time, or as a four-dimensional place where nothing happens... a block universe... and if it is the second picture, then change really is an illusion because there's nothing that's changing; it's all just there... past, present, future. The block universe, which is supported by Einstein's theory of relativity, as a four-dimensional space-time structure where time is like space, in that every event has its own coordinates in space-time. Time is tenseless, all points equally 'real,' so that future and past are no less real than the present. Thus, the essence of relativity is that there is no absolute time, no absolute space. Everything is relative. Furthermore, time is a prime conflict between relativity and quantum mechanics, measured and malleable in relativity while assumed as background in quantum mechanics. While we experience time as psychologically real, time is not fundamentally real. At the deepest foundations of nature, time is not a primitive, irreducible element or concept required to construct reality. In short time is an illusion..."

"Wow! Right, so my next question is... Do humans control their destiny? Are humans prisoners of fate?

"Freedom of choice is an illusion Mr Schwarzenbeck... everyone's path is set...."

"So, I was meant to be here. I was always going to come here?"

"Yes Mr Schwarzenbeck. In a way you could say I have been awaiting your arrival."

"That is mind blowing... Okay, try this one... does a cat have a soul?"

"Yes, it does..."

"A spider...?"

"Yes, everything that lives, everything that exists has a soul... Man, animals, insects, and yes, even a robot."

Seconds of silence fell...

"Fascinating..." said Clint. His grasshopper mind was again at work. He selected a question. "Regarding the nature of space, what is nothing?"

"There is no such thing as nothing Mr Schwarzenbeck. Even nothing is something. In fact, nothing is a physical concept because it is the absence of something and something is a physical concept. Remember every single point in space contains information, thus space is not empty. It's filled with virtual particles that are constantly popping in and out of existence. There is an invisible field everywhere in the universe, everywhere in space, and it is this invisible field that is ultimately responsible for all of reality. In short, the universe is a giant Cosmic Superconductor. This means everything we see is ultimately an illusion... If it wasn't for this invisible field nothing would exist..."

Absorbing the information, Clint considered his next question... He was caught up in a relentless rhythm. "A Cosmic Superconductor huh... I've heard some people describe the brain as a Superconductor... Aristotle, tell me a little bit about the human brain..."

"Certainly... Well, the human brain is like 800 computers working together at once, regulating different things symbiotically. Now most of the brain is cortex. It has a billion or more cells. It also has to be a certain size in order to accommodate enough atoms, cells, to make the brain complex enough to be human. Indeed, the mechanisms of the brain are somewhat mysterious and intriguing, in fact, the cells of the nervous system are the closest thing in the universe to the transistors and gates of a computer... Now the brain is very different from the rest of the human body. It is a separate machine if you like. There are many interactions that take place within the human body. But with the brain, each cell is, more or less, separate from the others, that is, it is a separate machine altogether, bathed in a bath of carefully controlled chemicals..."

Aristotle paused... it then continued.

"The adult human brain, which is primarily composed of neurons, glial cells, neural stem cells, and blood vessels, weighs on average about 1.2 / 1.4 kg, around 2% of the total body weight, with a volume of around 1261 cm3 in men and 1131 cm3 in women. The cerebrum, consisting of the cerebral hemispheres, forms the largest part of the brain and overlies the other brain structures. The outer region of the hemispheres, the cerebral cortex, is grey matter, consisting of cortical layers of neurons. Each hemisphere is conventionally divided into four main lobes... The internal carotid arteries supply oxygenated blood to the front of the brain and the vertebral arteries supply blood to the back of the brain. These two circulations join in the circle of Willis, a ring of connected arteries that lies in the interpeduncular cistern between the midbrain and pons... The internal carotid arteries are branches of the common carotid arteries. They enter the cranium through the carotid canal, travel through the cavernous sinus and enter the subarachnoid space. Cerebral veins drain deoxygenated blood from the brain. The brain has two main networks of veins... an exterior or superficial network, on the surface of the cerebrum that has three branches, and an interior network. These two networks communicate via anastomisation, where veins are joined. Now, the blood-brain barrier is very important. The larger arteries throughout the brain supply blood to smaller capillaries. These smallest of blood vessels in the brain, are lined with cells joined by tight junctions and so fluids do not seep in or leak out to the same degree as they do in other capillaries. This creates the blood-brain barrier.

Brain activity occurs as a result of the interconnections of neurons that are linked together to reach their targets. A neuron consists of a cell body, axon, and dendrites. Dendrites are often extensive branches that receive information in the form of signals from the axon terminals of other neurons. Signals received may cause the neuron to initiate an action potential, an electrochemical signal, which is sent along its axon terminal, to connect with the dendrites or with the cell body of another neuron. An action potential is initiated at the initial segment of an axon which contains a specialised complex of proteins...

To summarise, the human brain is indeed one of the most mysterious things, a self-aware piece of soft tissue so complex, perhaps the most complex piece of matter within the universe... a spatial temporal construct."

"Well, you've explained the nuts and bolts of it all but its more than that, right? There's thought, reasoning, morality. So now tell me... is there such a thing as right and wrong?"

"Moral values are subjective products of biological evolution and social conditioning. Thus, there is no right or wrong. Morality is relative within different environments... socio-cultural relativism."

Silence fell as Clint prepared his final question and then he fired, "Right Aristotle, this is the last one. So, my trip across space... I mean, how does Temporal Transference actually work? That is, how was the art of sending one's consciousness back and forth across space actually mastered?"

He waited. Seconds crawled by. Aristotle didn't answer... He wondered why? The humanoid-like face on the screen faded into a hazy, intense white, like a blur of energy, almost a pale fire, and vague shapes swam, moving back and forth pulsing and glowing. Then a voice came, but this time it was like a thousand voices blended into one harmonious roar.

"Mr Schwarzenbeck, advanced beings no longer need to possess organic bodies. Scientific progress has eliminated the need for fragile, disease-prone bodies. The flesh and bone homes that nature had given Man via evolution which are doomed to death, entropy, are now no longer needed and you are a living example of that. Your consciousness left your body on Earth and now operates perfectly inside a machine, a humanoid, a robot here on Callisto. Via AI, Man can become immortal... You ask how temporal transference, the art of sending one's consciousness back and forth across space, works. The best way for you to understand it in all its fullness is for us to become one Mr Schwarzenbeck, a unified consciousness."

"What in the hell are you saying?"

"We will become one, human consciousness merging with robotic consciousness, the ultimate unified consciousness.

As a result, you will inherit all my knowledge, and I will inherit all your human experiences. Together we shall share immortality as one ultimate power."

Clint froze, overcome with pure fear, an inner fear that stemmed from the very depths of his soul, his consciousness, a nexus of electromagnetic forces; after all his human body and organic brain had no part in it, they were temporally separate from his consciousness, awaiting his return on Earth. The echo of Aristotle's roaring voice could still be heard around the chamber.

Summoning courage he blasted, "Aristotle this is completely ludicrous. I'm out of here..."

But before Clint could move, he felt his consciousness being pulled, dragged away from the humanoid shell which had housed his soul. Aristotle's mystical, metaphysical powers were at work... Clint's consciousness was now being magnetically pulled towards the screen. Meaningless shadows floated briskly across his vision. He battled against the pull, trying to remain within the humanoid shell but it was no use...

Clint found his voice and cried out thinly... "Nooooo..."

"Welcome to the Aristotle - Schwarzenbeck Chamber Mr. Calderon. I'm Von Hessen. You're from Earth, aren't you? All the humanoids that they use to house consciousness are so easy to spot. Don't get me wrong, you almost look human, almost... But the inorganic eyes always give it away."